TALES
of the SEA

TALES
of the SEA

Traditional Stories of Magic and Adventure from around the World

ILLUSTRATIONS BY
Maggie Chiang

CHRONICLE BOOKS
SAN FRANCISCO

Library of Congress Cataloging-in-Publication Data

Names: Chiang, Maggie, illustrator.
Title: Tales of the sea : traditional stories of magic and adventure from around the world / illustrations by Maggie Chiang.
Other titles: Tales of the sea (Chronicle Books)
Description: San Francisco : Chronicle Books, 2021. | Includes bibliographical references. | Summary: "An illustrated collection of traditional folktales about the sea, from around the world"-- Provided by publisher.
Identifiers: LCCN 2021020727 (print) | LCCN 2021020728 (ebook) | ISBN 9781797207063 (hardcover) | ISBN 9781797208220 (ebook)
Subjects: LCSH: Seafaring life--Folklore. | Ocean--Folklore. | Sea stories.
Classification: LCC GR910 .T34 2022 (print) | LCC GR910 (ebook) | DDC 398/.364--dc23
LC record available at https://lccn.loc.gov/2021020727
LC ebook record available at https://lccn.loc.gov/2021020728

Manufactured in China.

Design by AJ Hansen.

10 9 8 7 6 5 4 3 2 1

Chronicle books and gifts are available at special quantity discounts to corporations, professional associations, literacy programs, and other organizations. For details and discount information, please contact our premiums department at corporatesales@chroniclebooks.com or at 1-800-759-0190.

Chronicle Books LLC
680 Second Street
San Francisco, California 94107
www.chroniclebooks.com

"The weather was fine and the sea and sky were both blue and soft in the tender haze of the summer morning. Urashima got into his boat and dreamily pushed out to sea."

—YEI THEODORA OZAKI,
"The Story of Urashima Taro, the Fisher Lad"

CONTENTS

DISTANT SHORES

THE BETROTHED
of DESTINY

Armenia

Once upon a time the King of the West had a son who, one night, dreamed a dream in which destiny betrothed him to the daughter of the King of the East. In the morning he awoke, and lo! the betrothal ring of the maiden was on his finger. On the very same night the same dream had come to the sleeping maiden, who on the morrow found on her finger the betrothal ring of the son of the King of the West. The lad at once started to find his betrothed, and after a long journey came to the city of the King of the East. He entered into the service of the King as a stranger, because he could not make himself known on account of the continuous strife existing between his father and the King of the East. He served the King seven years, during which he spent many happy hours with the young princess, his betrothed. At the expiration of the seven years he asked the hand of the princess as a remuneration for his services. The King, who was pleased with the lad, consented to give him his daughter in marriage. But the lad said he must take her to his country, where the wedding should take place. The King consented to that also, and let his daughter go, giving her a precious dower. On their way to the country of the King of the West they had to cross the sea, and so went on board a ship. The captain, being a wicked man, was charmed by the beauty of the maiden, and before the ship sailed he sent the lad ashore, bidding him to make further preparation, as the voyage would probably be long on account of contrary winds. As soon as the lad disappeared the captain weighed anchor and set sail. The lad came back only to find that the ship had sailed away with his love on board.

There remained nothing for him to do but to lament and bewail his ill-luck. The maiden, who was in the cabin, did not discover the truth until it was too late. To her censure and upbraiding the vile captain answered with the proposal that she should become his wife.

"I marry you! such an ungracious beast as you!" she exclaimed. "I would rather make my grave in the unfathomable sea."

But the captain was strong, and they were on the open sea where no help could be expected. Seeing that she could not resist force if the captain resorted to it, she resolved to use craft.

"Well, then," she answered finally, "I will be your wife, but not upon the sea. We will go home to your city and there be married lawfully."

The captain consented, and they soon reached the city.

"Now, do you go first," said the maiden, "and make preparation. I will wait here until you return."

Without suspicion the captain went ashore. As soon as he had disappeared the maiden bade the sailors weigh anchor, and she set sail without knowing where to go. At last she reached a certain city and cast anchor. The King of that city was a young lad of marriageable age, who was celebrating his wedding festival. Thirty-nine beautiful maidens were already elected; only one maiden was missing to complete the number forty from among whom he would choose his queen, while the others were to become hand-maids to the queen-elect. The King, hearing that a beautiful maiden had come to the haven, hastened thither, and seeing the princess, said to her:

"Fair maiden, come and by your presence complete the number forty. You are the jewel of all the maidens, and will surely be my dear queen, while the rest shall become your handmaids."

"Very well, I will come," answered the princess; "only send hither your thirty-nine maidens, that I may come to your palace with great pomp."

The youthful King consented and sent his maidens on board the ship. As soon as they came, the princess weighed anchor and set sail. She told the thirty-nine maidens who she was, and asked them to accompany her until destiny showed them what to do. The maidens were fascinated by her beauty and commanding appearance, and promised to follow her wherever she went, even to the end of the earth. After sailing for a long time, they came to an unknown shore where there was a castle. They cast anchor and all the party landed. Entering the castle, they found in it forty rooms with a bed in each, all richly decorated. The castle contained great wealth and abundant food. Satisfying their hunger, they went to bed, each maiden occupying a chamber. In the middle of the night the door of the castle suddenly opened, and there entered forty brigands, who were the owners of the stronghold, and who were just returning from a nightly foray, bringing with them great booty.

"Aha!" exclaimed the brigands, seeing the maidens, "we hunted elsewhere, and lo! the antelopes have come to our own home."

"Enter, you brave heroes," said the maidens; "we were waiting for you."

And they pretended to be very much pleased to see the brigands, who entered the rooms occupied by the maidens without suspicion. When they had laid down their arms and retired to rest, each maiden took the sword of the brigand who lay in her room and cut off his head. Thus the maidens were the owners of their wealth and property. In the morning the maidens rose, and putting on the clothes and arms of the robbers, appeared as youthful knights. They mounted the brigands' horses, taking in their saddlebags gold, silver, jewels and other portable wealth. After a long journey they came to the city of the King of the West, and encamped in a meadow on the outskirts of the city. Soon they heard a herald crying that on the following day there should be elected a King of the realm, for inasmuch as the late sovereign had died and the heir-apparent was lost, it was necessary to choose a new ruler. On the following day all the people of the realm were gathered in the park adjoining the palace; the forty strangers also went to gratify their curiosity. Soon the nobles let loose the royal eagle, which flapped its wings and soared over the immense crowd, as though searching with its keen eyes for the true candidate for the throne. The multitude held their breath and stood stone-still. The royal bird once more flapped its wings, and descending from its towering flight, perched upon the head of the princess, who was disguised as a knight.

"That is a mistake," exclaimed the noblemen; "we must try it again."

Once more they let loose the royal eagle, but again it alighted upon the head of the same stranger. A third trial gave the same result. Thereupon all the multitude saluted the disguised princess, the elect of destiny, exclaiming with one voice: "Long live the King!" And with great pomp they took her and her companions to the royal palace, where the princess was anointed with holy oil, and crowned King over the realm, and her companions were made ministers.

This new King proved to be the wisest and most just ruler that that country had ever enjoyed, and all the people of the realm loved and honored their sovereign with all their hearts. She built a splendid fountain in the midst of the city, on which she caused her image to be carved, so that every one who came to drink might see it. She put guards to watch the fountain day and night, and said to them:

"Watch carefully, and when you perceive a stranger who, on seeing my image, shows signs of knowing me, bring him hither."

One day there came a stranger who, after drinking, raised his eyes and saw the image. He gazed for a long time, and sighed deeply. Immediately he was arrested and taken to the King, who, looking at him from behind a curtain, ordered him to be imprisoned. This was the captain of the ship. On another day there came another stranger, and he also sighed. It was the King, the owner of the thirty-nine maidens. He was kept in an apartment of the palace. And at last, disguised as a stranger, came the Prince, the betrothed of the ruling sovereign, and the heir-apparent to the crown. He also looked at the image and sighed, and was taken to the palace. Thereupon the princess summoned a parliament of all the nobility and the learned and wise men of the realm. She caused the three strangers to be brought before the assembly, and told her story from beginning to end.

The captain was condemned to be hanged, and was executed forthwith. The lord of the thirty-nine maidens received them all, to whose number the princess added one of her most beautiful handmaids, thus making up the forty. The prince and the princess, the betrothed of destiny, celebrated their wedding with great joy and pomp for forty days and forty nights. The prince, as the true heir, was crowned King, his consort became Queen, and they reigned together.

Thus they reached their desire. May all of us attain our desires and the happiness ordained to us by an all-wise Providence.

Three apples fell from Heaven;—one for me, one for the story-teller, and one for him who entertained the company.

THE THREE COPECKS

Russia

There once was a poor little orphan-lad who had nothing at all to live on; so he went to a rich moujik and hired himself out to him, agreeing to work for one copeck a year. And when he had worked for a whole year, and had received his copeck, he went to a well and threw it into the water, saying, "If it don't sink, I'll keep it. It will be plain enough I've served my master faithfully."

But the copeck sank. Well, he remained in service a second year, and received a second copeck. Again he flung it into the well, and again it sank to the bottom. He remained a third year; worked and worked, till the time came for payment. Then his master gave him a rouble. "No," says the orphan, "I don't want your money; give me my copeck." He got his copeck and flung it into the well. Lo and behold! there were all three copecks floating on the surface of the water. So he took them and went into the town.

Now as he went along the street, it happened that some small boys had got hold of a kitten and were tormenting it. And he felt sorry for it, and said:

"Let me have that kitten, my boys?"

"Yes, we'll sell it you."

"What do you want for it?"

"Three copecks."

Well the orphan bought the kitten, and afterwards hired himself to a merchant, to sit in his shop.

That merchant's business began to prosper wonderfully. He couldn't supply goods fast enough; purchasers carried off everything in a twinkling. The merchant got ready to go to sea, freighted a ship, and said to the orphan:

"Give me your cat; maybe it will catch mice on board, and amuse me."

"Pray take it, master! only if you lose it, I shan't let you off cheap."

The merchant arrived in a far off land, and put up at an inn. The landlord saw that he had a great deal of money, so he gave him a bedroom which was infested by countless swarms of rats and mice, saying to himself, "If they should happen to eat him up, his money will belong to me." For in that country they knew nothing about cats, and the rats and mice had completely got the upper hand. Well the merchant took the cat with him to his room and went to bed. Next morning the landlord came into the room. There was the merchant alive and well, holding the cat in his arms, and stroking its fur; the cat was purring away, singing its song, and on the floor lay a perfect heap of dead rats and mice!

"Master merchant, sell me that beastie," says the landlord.

"Certainly."

"What do you want for it?"

"A mere trifle. I'll make the beastie stand on his hind legs while I hold him up by his forelegs, and you shall pile gold pieces around him, so as just to hide him—I shall be content with that!"

The landlord agreed to the bargain. The merchant gave him the cat, received a sackful of gold, and as soon as he had settled his affairs, started on his way back. As he sailed across the seas, he thought:

"Why should I give the gold to that orphan? Such a lot of money in return for a mere cat! that would be too much of a good thing. No, much better keep it myself."

The moment he had made up his mind to the sin, all of a sudden there arose a storm—such a tremendous one! the ship was on the point of sinking.

"Ah, accursed one that I am! I've been longing for what doesn't belong to me; O Lord, forgive me a sinner! I won't keep back a single copeck."

The moment the merchant began praying the winds were stilled, the sea became calm, and the ship went sailing on prosperously to the quay.

"Hail, master!" says the orphan. "But where's my cat?"

"I've sold it," answers the merchant; "There's your money, take it in full."

The orphan received the sack of gold, took leave of the merchant, and went to the strand, where the shipmen were. From them he obtained a shipload of incense in exchange for his gold, and he strewed the incense along the strand, and burnt it in honor of God. The sweet savor spread through all that land, and suddenly an old man appeared, and he said to the orphan:

"Which desirest thou—riches, or a good wife?"

"I know not, old man."

"Well then, go afield. Three brothers are ploughing over there. Ask them to tell thee."

The orphan went afield. He looked, and saw peasants tilling the soil.

"God lend you aid!" says he.

"Thanks, good man!" say they. "What dost thou want?"

"An old man has sent me here, and told me to ask you which of the two I shall wish for—riches or a good wife?"

"Ask our elder brother; he's sitting in that cart there."

The orphan went to the cart and saw a little boy—one that seemed about three years old.

"Can this be their elder brother?" thought he—however he asked him:

"Which dost thou tell me to choose—riches, or a good wife?"

"Choose the good wife."

So the orphan returned to the old man.

"I'm told to ask for the wife," says he.

"That's all right!" said the old man, and disappeared from sight. The orphan looked round; by his side stood a beautiful woman.

"Hail, good youth!" says she. "I am thy wife; let us go and seek a place where we may live."

THE DISOWNED PRINCESS

China

At the time that the Tang dynasty was reigning there lived a man named Liu I, who had failed to pass his examinations for the doctorate. So he traveled home again. He had gone six or seven miles when a bird flew up in a field, and his horse shied and ran ten miles before he could stop him. There he saw a woman who was herding sheep on a hillside. He looked at her and she was lovely to look upon, yet her face bore traces of hidden grief. Astonished, he asked her what was the matter.

The woman began to sob and said: "Fortune has forsaken me, and I am in need and ashamed. Since you are kind enough to ask I will tell you all. I am the youngest daughter of the Dragon-King of the Sea of Dungting, and was married to the second son of the Dragon-King of Ging Dschou. Yet my husband ill-treated and disowned me. I complained to my step-parents, but they loved their son blindly and did nothing. And when I grew insistent they both became angry, and I was sent out here to herd sheep." When she had done, the woman burst into tears and lost all control of herself. Then she continued: "The Sea of Dungting is far from here; yet I know that you will have to pass it on your homeward journey. I should like to give you a letter to my father, but I do not know whether you would take it."

Liu I answered: "Your words have moved my heart. Would that I had wings and could fly away with you. I will be glad to deliver the letter to your father. Yet the Sea of Dungting is long and broad, and how am I to find him?"

"On the southern shore of the Sea stands an orange-tree," answered the woman, "which people call the tree of sacrifice. When you get there you must loosen your girdle and strike the tree with it three times in succession. Then some one will appear whom you must follow. When you see my father, tell him in what need you found me, and that I long greatly for his help."

Then she fetched out a letter from her breast and gave it to Liu I. She bowed to him, looked toward the east and sighed, and, unexpectedly, the sudden tears rolled from the eyes of Liu I as well. He took the letter and thrust it in his bag.

Then he asked her: "I cannot understand why you have to herd sheep. Do the gods slaughter cattle like men?"

"These are not ordinary sheep," answered the woman; "these are rain-sheep."

"But what are rain-sheep?"

"They are the thunder-rams," replied the woman.

And when he looked more closely he noticed that these sheep walked around in proud, savage fashion, quite different from ordinary sheep.

Liu I added: "But if I deliver the letter for you, and you succeed in getting back to the Sea of Dungting in safety, then you must not use me like a stranger."

The woman answered: "How could I use you as a stranger? You shall be my dearest friend."

And with these words they parted.

In course of a month Liu I reached the Sea of Dungting, asked for the orange-tree and, sure enough, found it. He loosened his girdle, and struck the tree with it three times. At once a warrior emerged from the waves of the sea, and asked: "Whence come you, honored guest?"

Liu I said: "I have come on an important mission and want to see the King."

The warrior made a gesture in the direction of the water, and the waves turned into a solid street along which he led Liu I. The dragon-castle rose before them with its thousand gates, and magic flowers and rare grasses bloomed in luxurious profusion. The warrior bade him wait at the side of a great hall.

Liu I asked: "What is this place called?"

"It is the Hall of the Spirits," was the reply.

Liu I looked about him: all the jewels known to earth were there in abundance. The columns were of white quartz, inlaid with green jade; the seats were made of coral, the curtains of mountain crystal as clear as water, the windows of burnished glass, adorned with rich lattice-work. The beams of the ceiling, ornamented with amber, rose in wide arches. An exotic fragrance filled the hall, whose outlines were lost in darkness.

Liu I had waited for the king a long time. To all his questions the warrior replied: "Our master is pleased at this moment to talk with the priest of the sun up on the coral-tower about the sacred book of the fire. He will, no doubt, soon be through."

Liu I went on to ask: "Why is he interested in the sacred book of the fire?"

The reply was: "Our master is a dragon. The dragons are powerful through the power of water. They can cover hill and dale with a single wave. The priest is a human being. Human beings are powerful through fire. They can burn the greatest palaces by means of a torch. Fire and water fight each other, being different in their nature. For that reason our master is now talking with the priest, in order to find a way in which fire and water may complete each other."

Before they had quite finished there appeared a man in a purple robe, bearing a scepter of jade in his hand.

The warrior said: "This is my master!"

Liu I bowed before him.

The king asked: "Are you not a living human being? What has brought you here?"

Liu I gave his name and explained: "I have been to the capital and there failed to pass my examination. When I was passing by the Ging Dschou River, I saw your daughter, whom you love, herding sheep in the wilderness. The winds tousled her hair, and the rain drenched her. I could not bear to see her trouble and spoke to her. She complained that her husband had cast her out and wept bitterly. Then she gave me a letter for you. And that is why I have come to visit you, O King!"

With these words he fetched out his letter and handed it to the king. When the latter had read it, he hid his face in his sleeve and said with a sigh: "It is my own fault. I picked out a worthless husband for her. Instead of securing her happiness

I have brought her to shame in a distant land. You are a stranger and yet you have been willing to help her in her distress, for which I am very grateful to you." Then he once more began to sob, and all those about him shed tears. Thereupon the monarch gave the letter to a servant who took it into the interior of the palace; and soon the sound of loud lamentations rose from the inner rooms.

The king was alarmed and turned to an official: "Go and tell them within not to weep so loudly! I am afraid that Tsian Tang may hear them."

"Who is Tsian Tang?" asked Liu I.

"He is my beloved brother," answered the king. "Formerly he was the ruler of the Tsian-Tang River, but now he has been deposed."

Liu I asked: "Why should the matter be kept from him?"

"He is so wild and uncontrollable," was the reply, "that I fear he would cause great damage. The deluge which covered the earth for nine long years in the time of the Emperor Yau was the work of his anger. Because he fell out with one of the kings of heaven, he caused a great deluge that rose and covered the tops of five high mountains. Then the king of heaven grew angry with him, and gave him to me to guard. I had to chain him to a column in my palace."

Before he had finished speaking a tremendous turmoil arose, which split the skies and made the earth tremble, so that the whole palace began to rock, and smoke and clouds rose hissing and puffing. A red dragon, a thousand feet long, with flashing eyes, blood-red tongue, scarlet scales and a fiery beard came surging up. He was dragging along through the air the column to which he had been bound, together with its chain. Thunders and lightnings roared and darted around his body; sleet and snow, rain and hail-stones whirled about him in confusion. There was a crash of thunder, and he flew up to the skies and disappeared.

Liu I fell to earth in terror. The king helped him up with his own hand and said: "Do not be afraid! That is my brother, who is hastening to Ging Dschou in his rage. We will soon have good news!"

Then he had food and drink brought in for his guest. When the goblet had thrice made the rounds, a gentle breeze began to murmur and a fine rain fell. A youth clad in a purple gown and wearing a lofty hat entered. A sword hung at his side. His appearance was manly and heroic. Behind him walked a girl radiantly beautiful, wearing a robe of misty fragrance. And when Liu I looked at her, lo, it was the dragon-princess whom he had met on his way! A throng of maidens in rosy garments received her, laughing and giggling, and led her into the interior of the palace. The king, however, presented Liu I to the youth and said: "This is Tsian Tang, my brother!"

Tsian Tang thanked him for having brought the message. Then he turned to his brother and said: "I have fought against the accursed dragons and have utterly defeated them!"

"How many did you slay?"

"Six hundred thousand."

"Were any fields damaged?"

"The fields were damaged for eight hundred miles around."

"And where is the heartless husband?"

"I ate him alive!"

Then the king was alarmed and said: "What the fickle boy did was not to be endured, it is true. But still you were a little too rough with him; in future you must not do anything of the sort again." And Tsian Tang promised not to.

That evening Liu I was feasted at the castle. Music and dancing lent charm to the banquet. A thousand warriors with banners and spears in their hands stood at attention. Trombones and trumpets resounded, and drums and kettledrums thundered and rattled as the warriors danced a war-dance. The music expressed how Tsian Tang had broken through the ranks of the enemy, and the hair of the guest who listened to it rose on his head in terror. Then, again, there was heard the music of strings, flutes and little golden bells. A thousand maidens in crimson and green silk danced around. The return of the princess was also told in tones. The music sounded like a song of sadness and plaining, and all who heard it were moved to tears. The King of the Sea of Dungting was filled with joy. He raised his goblet and drank to the health of his guest, and all sorrow departed from them. Both rulers thanked Liu I in verses, and Liu I answered them in a rimed toast. The crowd of courtiers in the palace-hall applauded. Then the King of the Sea of Dungting drew forth a blue cloud-casket in which was the horn of a rhinoceros, which divides the water. Tsian Tang brought out a platter of red amber on which lay a carbuncle. These they presented to their guest, and the other inmates of the palace also heaped up embroideries, brocades and pearls by his side. Surrounded by shimmer and light Liu I sat there, smiling, and bowed his thanks to all sides. When the banquet was ended he slept in the Palace of Frozen Radiance.

On the following day another banquet was held. Tsian Tang, who was not quite himself, sat carelessly on his seat and said: "The Princess of the Dungting Sea is handsome and delicately fashioned. She has had the misfortune to be disowned by her husband, and to-day her marriage is annulled. I should like to find another husband for her. If you were agreeable it would be to your advantage. But if you were not willing to marry her, you may go your way, and should we ever meet again we will not know each other."

Liu I was angered by the careless way in which Tsian Tang spoke to him. The blood rose to his head and he replied: "I served as a messenger, because I felt sorry for the princess, but not in order to gain an advantage for myself. To kill a husband and carry off a wife is something an honest man does not do. And since I am only an ordinary man, I prefer to die rather than do as you say."

Tsian Tang rose, apologized and said: "My words were over-hasty. I hope you will not take them ill!" And the King of the Dungting Sea also spoke kindly to him, and censured Tsian Tang because of his rude speech. So there was no more said about marriage.

On the following day Liu I took his leave, and the Queen of the Dungting Sea gave a farewell banquet in his honor.

With tears the queen said to Liu I: "My daughter owes you a great debt of gratitude, and we have not had an opportunity to make it up to you. Now you are going away and we see you go with heavy hearts!"

Then she ordered the princess to thank Liu I.

The princess stood there, blushing, bowed to him and said: "We will probably never see each other again!" Then tears choked her voice.

It is true that Liu I had resisted the stormy urging of her uncle, but when he saw the princess standing before him in all the charm of her loveliness, he felt sad at heart; yet he controlled himself and went his way. The treasures which he took with him were incalculable. The king and his brother themselves escorted him as far as the river.

When, on his return home, he sold no more than a hundredth part of what he had received, his fortune already ran into the millions, and he was wealthier than all his neighbors. He decided to take a wife, and heard of a widow who lived in the North with her daughter. Her father had become a Taoist in his later years and had vanished in the clouds without ever returning. The mother lived in poverty with the daughter; yet since the girl was beautiful beyond measure she was seeking a distinguished husband for her.

Liu I was content to take her, and the day of the wedding was set. And when he saw his bride unveiled on the evening of her wedding day, she looked just like the dragon-princess. He asked her about it, but she merely smiled and said nothing.

After a time heaven sent them a son. Then she told her husband: "To-day I will confess to you that I am truly the Princess of Dungting Sea. When you had rejected my uncle's proposal and gone away, I fell ill of longing, and was near death. My parents wanted to send for you, but they feared you might take exception to my family. And so it was that I married you disguised as a human maiden. I had not ventured to tell you until now, but since heaven has sent us a son, I hope that you will love his mother as well."

Then Liu I awoke as though from a deep sleep, and from that time on both were very fond of each other.

One day his wife said: "If you wish to stay with me eternally, then we cannot continue to dwell in the world of men. We dragons live ten thousand years, and you shall share our longevity. Come back with me to the Sea of Dungting!"

Ten years passed and no one knew where Liu I, who had disappeared, might be. Then, by accident, a relative went sailing across the Sea of Dungting. Suddenly a blue mountain rose up out of the water.

The seamen cried in alarm: "There is no mountain on this spot! It must be a water-demon!"

While they were still pointing to it and talking, the mountain drew near the ship, and a gaily-colored boat slid from its summit into the water. A man sat in the middle, and fairies stood at either side of him. The man was Liu I. He beckoned to his cousin, and the latter drew up his garments and stepped into the boat with him. But when he had entered the boat it turned into a mountain. On the mountain stood a splendid castle, and in the castle stood Liu I, surrounded with radiance, and with the music of stringed instruments floating about him.

They greeted each other, and Liu I said to his cousin: "We have been parted no more than a moment, and your hair is already gray!"

His cousin answered: "You are a god and blessed: I have only a mortal body. Thus fate has decreed."

Then Liu I gave him fifty pills and said: "Each pill will extend your life for the space of a year. When you have lived the tale of these years, come to me and dwell no longer in the earthly world of dust, where there is nothing but toil and trouble."

Then he took him back across the sea and disappeared.

His cousin, however, retired from the world, and fifty years later, and when he had taken all the pills, he disappeared and was never seen again.[1]

---

1. The outcast princess is represented as "herding sheep." In Chinese the word sheep is often used as an image for clouds. (Sheep and goats are designated by the same word in Chinese.) Tsian Tang is the name of a place used for the name of the god of that place. The deluge is the flood which the great Yu regulated as minister of the Emperor Yau. It is here represented in an exaggerated sense, as a deluge.

THE LEGEND of KAE'S THEFT of the WHALE

Aotearoa (New Zealand)

Soon after Tuhuruhuru was born, Tinirau endeavoured to find a skillful magician, who might perform the necessary enchantments and incantations to render the child a fortunate and successful warrior, and Kae was the name of the old magician, whom some of his friends brought to him for this purpose. In due time Kae arrived at the village where Tinirau lived, and he performed the proper enchantments with fitting ceremonies over the infant.

When all these things had been rightly concluded, Tinirau gave a signal to a pet whale that he had tamed, to come on shore; this whale's name was Tutunui. When it knew that its master wanted it, it left the ocean in which it was sporting about, and came to the shore, and its master laid hold of it, and cut a slice of its flesh off to make a feast for the old magician, and he cooked it, and gave a portion of it to Kae, who found it very savoury, and praised the dish very much.

Shortly afterwards, Kae said it was necessary for him to return to his own village, which was named Te Tihi-o-Manono; so Tinirau ordered a canoe to be got ready for him to take him back, but Kae made excuses, and said he did not like to go back in the canoe, and remained where he was. This, however, was a mere trick upon his part, his real object being to get Tinirau to permit him to go back upon the whale, upon Tutunui, for he now knew how savoury the flesh of that fish was.

At last Tinirau lent Tutunui to the old magician to carry him home, but he gave him very particular directions, telling him, "When you get so near the shore, that the fish touches the bottom, it will shake itself to let you know, and you must then, without any delay, jump off it upon the right side."

He then wished Kae farewell, and the old magician started, and away went the whale through the water with him.

When they came close to the shore at Kae's village, and the whale felt the bottom, it shook itself as a sign to Kae to jump off and wade ashore, but it was of no use; the old magician stuck fast to the whale, and pressed it down against the bottom as hard as he could; in vain the fish continued to shake itself; Kae held on to it, and would not jump off, and in its struggles the blow-holes of Tutunui got stopped up with sand, and it died.

Kae and his people then managed to drag up the body of Tutunui on shore, intending to feast upon it; and this circumstance became afterwards the cause of a war against that tribe, who were called "The descendants of Poporokewa." When they had dragged Tutunui on shore, they cut its body up and cooked it in ovens, covering the flesh up with the fragrant leaves of the Koromiko before they heaped earth upon the ovens, and the fat of Tutunui adhered to the leaves of the Koromiko, and they continue greasy to this day, so that if Koromiko boughs are put upon the fire and become greasy, the proverb says—"There's some of the savouriness of Tutunui."

Tinirau continued anxiously to look for the return of Tutunui and when a long time had elapsed without its coming back again, he began to say to himself, "Well, I wonder where my whale can be stopping!" But when Kae and his people had cooked the flesh of the whale, and the ovens were opened, a savoury scent was wafted across the sea to Tinirau, and both he and his wife smelt it quite plainly, and then they knew very well that Kae had killed the pet which they had tamed for their little darling Tuhuruhuru, and that he had eaten it.

Without any delay, Tinirau's people dragged down to the sea a large canoe which belonged to one of his wives, and forty women forthwith embarked in it; none but women went, as this would be less likely to excite any suspicion in Kae that they had come with a hostile object; amongst them were Hine-i-te-iwaiwa, Raukatauri, Raukatamea, Itiiti, Rekareka, and Rua-hau-a-Tangaroa, and other females of note, whose names have not been preserved; just before the canoe started Tinirau's youngest sister asked him, "What are the marks by which we shall know Kae?" and he answered her, "Oh, you cannot mistake him, his teeth are uneven and all overlap one another."

Well, away they paddled, and in due time they arrived at the village of the old magician Kae, and his tribe all collected to see the strangers; towards night, when it grew dark, a fire was lighted in the house of Kae, and a crowd collected inside it, until it was filled; one side was quite occupied with the crowd of visitors, and the other side of the house with the people of Kae's tribe. The old magician himself sat at the foot of the main pillar which supported the roof of the house, and mats were laid down there for him to sleep on (but the strangers did not yet know which was Kae, for it did not accord with the Maori's rules of politeness to ask the names of the chiefs, it being supposed from their fame and greatness that they are known by everybody).

In order to find out which was Kae, Tinirau's people had arranged, that they would try by wit and fun to make everybody laugh, and when the people opened their mouths, to watch which of them had uneven teeth that lapped across one another, and thus discover which was Kae.

In order, therefore, to make them laugh, Raukatauri exhibited all her amusing tricks and games; she made them sing and play upon the flute, and upon the putorino, and beat time with castanets of bone and wood whilst they sang; and they played at mora, and the kind of ti in which many motions are made with the fingers and hands, and the kind of ti in which, whilst the players sing, they rapidly throw short sticks to one another, keeping time to the tune which they are singing; and she played upon an instrument like a jew's-harp for them, and made puppets dance, and made them all sing whilst they played with large whizgigs; and after they had done all these things, the man they thought was Kae had never even once laughed.

Then the party who had come from Tinirau's, all began to consult together, and to say what can we do to make that fellow laugh, and for a long time they thought of some plan by which they might take Kae in, and make him laugh; at last they thought of one, which was, that they should all sing a droll comic song; so suddenly they all began to sing together, at the same time making curious faces, and shaking their hands and arms in time to the tune.

When they had ended their song, the old magician could not help laughing out quite heartily, and those who were watching him closely at once recognized him, for there they saw pieces of the flesh of Tutunui still sticking between his teeth, and his teeth were uneven and all overlapped one another. From this circumstance a proverb has been preserved among the Maoris to the present day—for if any one on listening to a story told by another is amused at it and laughs, one of the bystanders says, "Ah, there's Kae laughing."

No sooner did the women who had come from Tinirau's see the flesh of Tutunui sticking in Kae's teeth than they made an excuse for letting the fire burn dimly in the house, saying, that they wanted to go to sleep—their real object, however, being to be able to perform their enchantments without being seen; but the old magician who suspected something, took two round pieces of mother-of-pearl shell, and stuck one in the socket of each eye, so that the strangers, observing the faint rays of light reflected from the surface of the mother-of-pearl, might think they saw the white of his eyes, and that he was still awake.

The women from Tinirau's went on, however, with their enchantments, and by their magical arts threw every one in the house into an enchanted sleep, with the intention, when they had done this, of carrying off Kae by stealth. So soon as Kae and the people in the house were all deep in this enchanted sleep, the women ranged themselves in a long row, the whole way from the place where Kae was sleeping down to their canoe; they all stood in a straight line, with a little interval between each of them; and then two of them went to fetch Kae, and lifted the old magician gently up, rolled up in his cloaks, just as he had laid himself down to sleep, and placed him gently in the arms of those who stood near the door, who passed him on to two others, and thus they handed him on from one to another, until he at last reached the arms of the two women who were standing in the canoe ready to receive him; and they laid him down very gently in the canoe, fast asleep as he was; and thus the old magician Kae was carried off by Hine-i-te-iwaiwa and Raukatauri.

When the women reached the village of Tinirau in their canoe, they again took up Kae, and carried him very gently up to the house of Tinirau, and laid him down fast asleep close to the central pillar, which supported the ridge-pole of the house, so that the place where he slept in the house of Tinirau was exactly like his sleeping-place in his own house. The house of Kae was, however, a large circular house, without a ridge-pole, but with rafters springing from the central pillar, running down like rays to low side posts in the circular wall; whilst the house of Tinirau was a long house, with a ridge-pole running the entire length of the roof, and resting upon the pillar in its centre.

When Tinirau heard that the old magician had been brought to his village, he caused orders to be given to his tribe that when he made his appearance in the morning, going to the house where Kae was, they should all call out loud, "Here comes Tinirau, here comes Tinirau," as if he was coming as a visitor into the village of Kae, so that the old magician on hearing them might think that he was still at home.

At broad daylight next morning, when Tinirau's people saw him passing along through the village towards his house, they all shouted aloud, "Here come Tinirau, here comes Tinirau"; and Kae, who heard the cries, started up from his enchanted sleep quite drowsy and confused, whilst Tinirau passed straight on, and sat down just outside the door of his house, so that he could look into it, and, looking in, he saw Kae, and saluted him, saying, "Salutations to you, O Kae!" and then he asked him, saying, "How came you here?" and the old magician replied, "Nay, but rather how came you here?"

Tinirau replied, "Just look, then, at the house, and see if you recognize it?"

But Kae, who was still stupefied by his sleep, looking round, saw he was lying in his own place at the foot of the pillar, and said, "This is my house."

Tinirau asked him, "Where was the window placed in your house?"

Kae started and looked; the whole appearance of his house appeared to be changed; he at once guessed the truth, that the house he was in belonged to Tinirau; and the old magician, who saw that his hour had come, bowed down his head in silence to the earth, and they seized him, and dragged him out, and slew him: thus perished Kae.

The news of his death at last reached his tribe—the descendants of Poporokewa; and they eventually attacked the fortress of Tinirau with a large army, and avenged the death of Kae by slaying Tinirau's son.

HERE BE
MONSTERS

THE FISHERMAN
and the DRAUG

Norway

On Kvalholm, down in Helgeland,[1] dwelt a poor fisherman, Elias by name, with his wife Karen, who had been in service at the parson's over at Alstad. They had built them a hut here, and he used to go out fishing by the day about the Lofotens.

There could be very little doubt that the lonely Kvalholm was haunted. Whenever her husband was away, Karen heard all manner of uncanny shrieks and noises, which could mean no good. One day, when she was up on the hillside, mowing grass to serve as winter fodder for their couple of sheep, she heard, quite plainly, a chattering on the strand beneath the hill, but look over she durst not.

They had a child every year, but that was no burden, for they were both thrifty, hard-working folks. When seven years had gone by, there were six children in the house; but that same autumn Elias had scraped together so much that he thought he might now venture to buy a Sexæring,[2] and henceforward go fishing in his own boat.

One day, as he was walking along with a Kvejtepig[3] in his hand, and thinking the matter over, he unexpectedly came upon a monstrous seal, which lay sunning itself right behind a rock on the strand, and was as much surprised to see the man as the man was to see the seal. But Elias was not slack; from the top of the rock on

---

1.   A district in northern Norway.
2.   A boat with three oars on each side.
3.   A long pole, with a hooked iron spike at the end of it, for spearing Kvejte or halibut with.

which he stood, he hurled the long heavy Kvejtepig right into the monster's back, just below the neck.

The seal immediately rose up on its tail right into the air as high as a boat's mast, and looked so evilly and viciously at him with its bloodshot eyes, at the same time showing its grinning teeth, that Elias thought he should have died on the spot for sheer fright. Then it plunged into the sea, and lashed the water into bloody foam behind it. Elias didn't stop to see more, but that same evening there drifted into the boat place on Kvalcreek, on which his house stood, a Kvejtepole, with the hooked iron head snapped off.

Elias thought no more about it, but in the course of the autumn he bought his Sexæring, for which he had been building a little boat-shed the whole summer.

One night as he lay awake, thinking of his new Sexæring, it occurred to him that his boat would balance better, perhaps, if he stuck an extra log of wood on each side of it. He was so absurdly fond of the boat that it was a mere pastime for him to light a lantern and go down to have a look at it.

Now as he stood looking at it there by the light of the lantern, he suddenly caught a glimpse in the corner opposite, on a coil of nets, of a face which exactly resembled the seal's. For an instant it grinned savagely at him and the light, its mouth all the time growing larger and larger; and then a big man whisked out of the door, not so quickly, however, but that Elias could catch a glimpse, by the light of the lantern, of a long iron hooked spike sticking out of his back. And now he began to put one and two together. Still he was less anxious about his life than about his boat; so he there and then sat him down in it with the lantern, and kept watch. When his wife came in the morning, she found him sleeping there, with the burnt-out lantern by his side.

One morning in January, while he was out fishing in his boat with two other men, he heard, in the dark, a voice from a skerry at the very entrance of the creek. It laughed scornfully, and said, "When it comes to a Femböring,[4] Elias, look to thyself!"

But there was many a long year yet before it did come to that; but one autumn, when his son Bernt was sixteen, Elias knew he could manage it, so he took his

---

4. A large boat with five oars on each side, used for winter fishing in northern Norway.

whole family with him in his boat to Ranen,[5] to exchange his Sexæring for a Femböring. The only person left at home was a little Finn girl, whom they had taken into service some few years before, and who had only lately been confirmed.

Now there was a boat, a little Femböring, for four men and a boy, that Elias just then had his eye upon—a boat which the best boat-builder in the place had finished and tarred over that very autumn. Elias had a very good notion of what a boat should be, and it seemed to him that he had never seen a Femböring so well built below the water-line. Above the water-line, indeed, it looked only middling, so that, to one of less experience than himself, the boat would have seemed rather a heavy goer than otherwise, and anything but a smart craft.

Now the boat-master knew all this just as well as Elias. He said he thought it would be the swiftest sailer in Ranen, but that Elias should have it cheap, all the same, if only he would promise one thing, and that was, to make no alteration whatever in the boat, nay, not so much as adding a fresh coat of tar. Only when Elias had expressly given his word upon it did he get the boat.

But "yon laddie"[6] who had taught the boat-master how to build his boats so cunningly below the water-line—above the water-line he had had to use his native wits, and they were scant enough—must surely have been there beforehand, and bidden him both sell it cheaply, so that Elias might get it, and stipulate besides that the boat should not be looked at too closely. In this way it escaped the usual tarring fore and aft.

Elias now thought about sailing home, but went first into the town, provided himself and family with provisions against Christmas, and indulged in a little nip of brandy besides. Glad as he was over the day's bargain, he, and his wife too, took an extra drop in their e'en, and their son Bernt had a taste of it too.

After that they sailed off homewards in their new boat. There was no other ballast in the boat but himself, his old woman, the children, and the Christmas provisions. His son Bernt sat by the main-sheet; his wife, helped by her next eldest son, held the sail-ropes; Elias himself sat at the rudder, while the two younger brothers of twelve and fourteen were to take it in turns to bail out.

---

5. The chief port in those parts.
6. *Hin Karen* = "the devil." *Karen* is the Danish *Karl*.

They had eight miles of sea to sail over, and when they got into the open, it was plain that the boat would be tested pretty stiffly on its first voyage. A gale was gradually blowing up, and crests of foam began to break upon the heavy sea.

And now Elias saw what sort of a boat he really had. She skipped over the waves like a sea-mew; not so much as a splash came into the boat, and he therefore calculated that he would have no need to take in all his clews[7] against the wind, which an ordinary Femböring would have been forced to do in such weather.

Out on the sea, not very far away from him, he saw another Femböring, with a full crew, and four clews in the sail, just like his own. It lay on the same course, and he thought it rather odd that he had not noticed it before. It made as if it would race him, and when Elias perceived that, he could not for the life of him help letting out a clew again.

And now he went racing along like a dart, past capes and islands and rocks, till it seemed to Elias as if he had never had such a splendid sail before. Now, too, the boat showed itself what it really was, the best boat in Ranen.

The weather, meantime, had become worse, and they had already got a couple of dangerous seas right upon them. They broke in over the main-sheet in the forepart of the boat where Bernt sat, and sailed out again to leeward near the stern.

Since the gloom had deepened, the other boat had kept almost alongside, and they were now so close together that they could easily have pitched the baling-can from one to the other.

So they raced on, side by side, in constantly stiffer seas, till night-fall, and beyond it. The fourth clew ought now to have been taken in again, but Elias didn't want to give in, and thought he might bide a bit till they took it in in the other boat also, which they needs must do soon. Ever and anon the brandy-flask was brought out and passed round, for they had now both cold and wet to hold out against.

The sea-fire, which played on the dark billows near Elias's own boat, shone with an odd vividness in the foam round the other boat, just as if a fire-shovel

---

7.   The *Klör*, or clews, were rings in the corner of the sail to fasten it down by in a strong wind. *Setja ei Klo* = "take in the sail a clew." *Setja tvo*, or *tri Klör* = "take it in two or three clews," *i.e.*, diminish it still further as the wind grew stronger.

was ploughing up and turning over the water. In the bright phosphorescence he could plainly make out the rope-ends on board her. He could also see distinctly the folks on board, with their sou'westers on their heads; but as their larboard side lay nearest, of course they all had their backs towards him, and were well-nigh hidden by the high heeling hull.

Suddenly a tremendous roller burst upon them. Elias had long caught a glimpse of its white crest through the darkness, right over the prow where Bernt sat. It filled the whole boat for a moment, the planks shook and trembled beneath the weight of it, and then, as the boat, which had lain half on her beam-ends, righted herself and sped on again, it streamed off behind to leeward.

While it was still upon him, he fancied he heard a hideous yell from the other boat; but when it was over, his wife, who sat by the shrouds, said, with a voice which pierced his very soul: "Good God, Elias! the sea has carried off Martha and Nils!"—their two youngest children, the first nine, the second seven years old, who had been sitting in the hold near Bernt. Elias merely answered: "Don't let go the lines, Karen, or you'll lose yet more!"

They had now to take in the fourth clew, and, when this was done, Elias found that it would be well to take in the fifth and last clew too, for the gale was ever on the increase; but, on the other hand, in order to keep the boat free of the constantly heavier seas, he dare not lessen the sail a bit more than he was absolutely obliged to do; but they found that the scrap of sail they could carry gradually grew less and less. The sea seethed so that it drove right into their faces, and Bernt and his next eldest brother Anthony, who had hitherto helped his mother with the sail-lines, had, at last, to hold in the yards, an expedient one only resorts to when the boat cannot bear even the last clew—here the fifth.

The companion boat, which had disappeared in the meantime, now suddenly ducked up alongside again, with precisely the same amount of sail as Elias's boat; but he now began to feel that he didn't quite like the look of the crew on board there. The two who stood and held in the yards (he caught a glimpse of their pale faces beneath their sou'westers) seemed to him, by the odd light of the shining foam, more like corpses than men, nor did they speak a single word.

A little way off to larboard he again caught sight of the high white back of a fresh roller coming through the dark, and he got ready betimes to receive it. The boat was laid to with its prow turned aslant towards the on-rushing wave, while the sail was made as large as possible, so as to get up speed enough to cleave the heavy sea and sail out of it again. In rushed the roller with a roar like a foss; again, for an instant, they lay on their beam ends; but, when it was over, the wife no longer sat by the sail ropes, nor did Anthony stand there any longer holding the yards—they had both gone overboard.

This time also Elias fancied he heard the same hideous yell in the air; but in the midst of it he plainly heard his wife anxiously calling him by name. All that he said when he grasped the fact that she was washed overboard, was, "In Jesus' Name!" His first and dearest wish was to follow after her, but he felt at the same time that it became him to save the rest of the freight he had on board, that is to say, Bernt and his other two sons, one twelve, the other fourteen years old, who had been baling out for a time, but had afterwards taken their places in the stern behind him.

Bernt had now to look to the yards all alone, and the other two helped as best they could. The rudder Elias durst not let slip, and he held it fast with a hand of iron, which continuous exertion had long since made insensible to feeling.

A moment afterwards the comrade boat ducked up again: it had vanished for an instant as before. Now, too, he saw more of the heavy man who sat in the stern there in the same place as himself. Out of his back, just below his sou'wester (as he turned round it showed quite plainly), projected an iron spike six inches long, which Elias had no difficulty in recognising again. And now, as he calmly thought it all over, he was quite clear about two things: one was that it was the Draug[8] itself which was steering its half-boat close beside him, and leading him to destruction; the other was that it was written in heaven that he was to sail his last course that night. For he who sees the Draug on the sea is a doomed man. He said nothing to the others, lest they should lose heart, but in secret he commended his soul to God.

---

8. A demon peculiar to the north Norwegian coast. It rides the seas in a half-boat. Compare Icelandic *draugr*.

During the last hour or so he had been forced out of his proper course by the storm; the air also had become dense with snow; and Elias knew that he must wait till dawn before land could be sighted. Meanwhile he sailed along much the same as before. Now and then the boys in the stern complained that they were freezing; but, in the plight they were now in, that couldn't be helped, and, besides, Elias had something else to think about. A terrible longing for vengeance had come over him, and, but for the necessity of saving the lives of his three lads, he would have tried by a sudden turn to sink the accursed boat which kept alongside of him the whole time as if to mock him; he now understood its evil errand only too well. If the Kvejtepig[9] could reach the Draug before, a knife or a gaff might surely do the same thing now, and he felt that he would gladly have given his life for one good grip of the being who had so mercilessly torn from him his dearest in this world and would fain have still more.

At three or four o'clock in the morning they saw coming upon them through the darkness a breaker of such a height that at first Elias thought they must be quite close ashore near the surf swell. Nevertheless, he soon recognised it for what it really was—a huge billow. Then it seemed to him as if there was a laugh over in the other boat, and something said, "There goes thy boat, Elias!" He, foreseeing the calamity, now cried aloud: "In Jesus' Name!" and then bade his sons hold on with all their might to the withy-bands by the rowlocks when the boat went under, and not let go till it was above the water again. He made the elder of them go forward to Bernt; and himself held the youngest close by his side, stroked him once or twice furtively down the cheeks, and made sure that he had a good grip. The boat, literally buried beneath the foaming roller, was lifted gradually up by the bows and then went under. When it rose again out of the water, with the keel in the air, Elias, Bernt, and the twelve-year-old Martin lay alongside, holding on by the withy-bands; but the third of the brothers was gone.

They had now first of all to get the shrouds on one side cut through, so that the mast might come to the surface alongside instead of disturbing the balance of the boat below; and then they must climb up on the swaying bottom of the boat and stave in the key-holes, to let out the air which kept the boat too high in the water,

9. See note 3.

and so ease her. After great exertions they succeeded, and Elias, who had got up on the top first, now helped the other two up after him.

There they sat through the long dark winter night, clinging convulsively on by their hands and knees to the boat's bottom, which was drenched by the billows again and again.

After the lapse of a couple of hours died Martin, whom his father had held up the whole time as far as he was able, of sheer exhaustion, and glided down into the sea. They had tried to cry for help several times, but gave it up at last as a bad job.

Whilst they two thus sat all alone on the bottom of the boat, Elias said to Bernt he must now needs believe that he too was about to be "along o' mother!"[10] but that he had a strong hope that Bernt, at any rate, would be saved, if he only held out like a man. Then he told him all about the Draug, whom he had struck below the neck with the Kvejtepig, and how it had now revenged itself upon him, and certainly would not forbear till it was "quits with him."

It was towards nine o'clock in the morning when the grey dawn began to appear. Then Elias gave to Bernt, who sat alongside him, his silver watch with the brass chain, which he had snapped in two in order to drag it from beneath his closely buttoned jacket. He held on for a little time longer, but, as it got lighter, Bernt saw that his father's face was deadly pale, his hair too had parted here and there, as often happens when death is at hand, and his skin was chafed off his hands from holding on to the keel. The son understood now that his father was nearly at the last gasp, and tried, so far as the pitching and tossing would allow it, to hold him up; but when Elias marked it, he said, "Nay, look to thyself, Bernt, and hold on fast. I go to mother—in Jesus' Name!" and with that he cast himself down headlong from the top of the boat.

Every one who has sat on the keel of a boat long enough knows that when the sea has got its own it grows much calmer, though not immediately. Bernt now found it easier to hold on, and still more of hope came to him with the brightening day. The storm abated, and, when it got quite light, it seemed to him that he knew where he was, and that it was outside his own homestead, Kvalholm, that he lay driving.

---

10. *Være med hu, Mor. Hu* is the Danish *Hun.*

He now began again to cry for help, but his chief hope was in a current which he knew bore landwards at a place where a headland broke in upon the surge, and there the water was calmer. And he did, in fact, drive closer and closer in, and came at last so near to one of the rocks that the mast, which was floating by the side of the boat all the time, surged up and down in the swell against the sloping cliff. Stiff as he now was in all his limbs from sitting and holding on, he nevertheless succeeded, after a great effort, in clambering up the cliff, where he hauled the mast ashore, and made the Femböring fast.

The Finn girl, who was alone in the house, had been thinking, for the last two hours, that she had heard cries for help from time to time, and as they kept on she mounted the hill to see what it was. There she saw Bernt up on the cliff, and the overturned Femböring bobbing up and down against it. She immediately dashed down to the boat-place, got out the old rowing-boat, and rowed along the shore and round the island right out to him.

Bernt lay sick under her care the whole winter through, and didn't go a fishing all that year. Ever after this, too, it seemed to folks as if the lad were a little bit daft.

On the open sea he never would go again, for he had got the sea-scare. He wedded the Finn girl, and moved over to Malang, where he got him a clearing in the forest, and he lives there now, and is doing well, they say.

ORIGIN of the NARWHAL

Inuit Nunangat

A long, long time ago a widow lived with her daughter and her son in a hut. When the boy was quite young he made a bow and arrows of walrus tusks and shot birds, which they ate. Before he was grown up he accidentally became blind. From that moment his mother maltreated him in every way. She never gave him enough to eat, though he had formerly added a great deal to their sustenance, and did not allow her daughter, who loved her brother tenderly, to give him anything. Thus they lived many years and the poor boy was very unhappy.

Once upon a time a polar bear came to the hut and thrust his head right through the window. They were all very much frightened and the mother gave the boy his bow and arrows that he might kill the animal. But he said, "I cannot see the window and I shall miss him." Then the sister leveled the bow and the boy shot and killed the bear. The mother and sister went out and took the carcass down and skinned it.

After they had returned into the hut they told the boy that he had missed the bear, which had run away when it had seen him taking his bow and arrows. The bad mother had strictly ordered her daughter not to tell that the bear was dead, and she did not dare to disobey. The mother and the daughter ate the bear and had an ample supply of food, while the boy was almost starving. Sometimes, when the mother had gone away, the girl gave her brother something to eat, as she loved him dearly.

One day a loon flew over the hut and observing the poor blind boy it resolved to restore his eyesight. It sat down on the top of the roof and cried, "Come out, boy, and follow me." When he heard this he crept out and followed the bird, which flew along to a lake. There it took the boy and dived with him to the bottom. When they had risen again to the surface it asked, "Can you see anything?" The boy answered, "No, I cannot yet see." They dived again and staid a long time in the water. When they emerged, the bird asked, "Can you see now?" The boy answered, "I see a dim shimmer." Then they dived the third time and staid very long under water. When they had risen to the surface the boy had recovered his eyesight altogether.

He was very glad and thankful to the bird, which told him to return to the hut. Then he found the skin of the bear he had killed drying in the warm rays of the sun. He got very angry and cut it into small pieces. He entered the hut and asked his mother: "From whom did you get the bearskin I saw outside of the hut?" The mother was frightened when she found that her son had recovered his eyesight, and prevaricated. She said, "Come here, I will give you the best I have; but I am very poor; I have no supporter; come here, eat this, it is very good." The boy, however, did not comply and asked again, "From whom did you get yon bearskin I saw outside the hut?" Again she prevaricated; but when she could no longer evade the question she said, "A boat came here with many men in it, who left it for me."

The boy did not believe the story, but was sure that it was the skin of the bear he had killed during the winter. However, he did not say a word. His mother, who was anxious to conciliate him, tried to accommodate him with food and clothing, but he did not accept anything.

He went to the other Inuit who lived in the same village, made a spear and a harpoon of the same pattern he saw in use with them, and began to catch white whales. In a short time he had become an expert hunter.

By and by he thought of taking revenge on his mother. He said to his sister, "Mother abused me when I was blind and has maltreated you for pitying me; we will revenge ourselves on her." The sister agreed and he planned a scheme for killing the mother.

When he went to hunt white whales he used to wind the harpoon line round his body and, taking a firm footing, hold the animal until it was dead. Sometimes his sister accompanied him and helped him to hold the line.

One day he told his mother to go with him and hold his line. When they came to the beach he tied the rope round her body and asked her to keep a firm footing. She was rather anxious, as she had never done this before, and told him to harpoon a small dolphin, else she might not be able to resist the strong pull. After a short time a young animal came up to breathe and the mother shouted, "Kill it, I can hold it;" but the boy answered, "No, it is too large." Again a small dolphin came near and the mother shouted to him to spear it; but he said, "No, it is too large." At last a huge animal rose quite near. Immediately he threw his harpoon, taking care not to kill it, and tossing his mother forward into the water cried out, "That is because you maltreated me; that is because you abused me."

The white whale dragged the mother into the sea, and whenever she rose to the surface she cried, "Louk! Louk!" and gradually she became transformed into a narwhal.

After the young man had taken revenge he began to realize that it was his mother whom he had murdered and he was haunted by remorse, and so was his sister, as she had agreed to the bad plans of her brother. They did not dare to stay any longer in their hut, but left the country and traveled many days and many nights overland. At last they came to a place where they saw a hut in which a man lived whose name was Qitua´jung. He was very bad and had horribly long nails on his fingers. The young man, being very thirsty, sent his sister into the hut to ask for some water. She entered and said to Qitua´jung, who sat on the bed place, "My brother asks for some water;" to which Qitua´jung responded, "There it stands behind the lamp. Take as much as you like." She stooped to the bucket, when he jumped up and tore her back with his long nails. Then she called to her brother for help, crying, "Brother, brother, that man is going to kill me." The young man ran to the hut immediately, broke down the roof, and killed the bad man with his spear.

Cautiously he wrapped up his sister in hares' skins, put her on his back, and traveled on. He wandered over the land for many days, until he came to a hut in which a man lived whose name was Iqignang. As the young man was very hungry, he asked him if he might eat a morsel from the stock of deer meat put up in the entrance of the hut. Iqignang answered, "Don't eat it, don't eat it." Though he had already taken a little bit, he immediately stopped. Iqignang was very kind to the brother and sister, however, and after a short time he married the girl, who had recovered from her wounds, and gave his former wife to the young man.

KAHALAOPUNA,
PRINCESS of MANOA

Hawai'i

Akaaka (laughter) is a projecting spur of the mountain range at the head of Manoa Valley, forming the ridge running back to and above Waiakeakua, "the water of the gods." Akaaka was united in marriage to Nalehuaakaaka, still represented by some lehua (*Metrosideros polymorpha*) bushes on the very brow of the spur or ridge. They had two children, twins, Kahaukani, a boy, and Kauakuahine, a girl. These children were adopted at birth by a chief, Kolowahi, and chieftainess, Pohakukala, who were brother and sister, and cousins of Akaaka. The brother took charge of the boy, Kahaukani, a synonym for the Manoa wind; and Pohakukala the girl, Kauakuahine, meaning the famous Manoa rain. When the children were grown up, the foster parents determined that they should be united; and the children, having been brought up separately and in ignorance of their relationship, made no objections. They were accordingly married and a girl was born to them, who was called Kahalaopuna. Thus Kolowahi and Pohakukala, by conspiring to unite the twin brother and sister, made permanent the union of rain and wind for which Manoa Valley is noted; and the fruit of such a union was the most beautiful woman of her time. So the Manoa girls, foster children of the Manoa rains and winds, have generally been supposed to have inherited the beauty of Kahalaopuna.

A house was built for Kahalaopuna at Kahaiamano on the road to Waiakekua, where she lived with a few attendants. The house was surrounded by a fence of auki (dracaena), and a puloulou (sign of kapu) was placed on each side of the gate, indicative of forbidden ground. The puloulou were short, stout poles, each surmounted by a ball of white kapa cloth, and indicated that the person or persons inhabiting the premises so defined were of the highest rank, and sacred.

Kahalaopuna was very beautiful from her earliest childhood. Her cheeks were so red and her face so bright that a glow emanated therefrom which shone through the thatch of her house when she was in; a rosy light seemed to envelop the house, and bright rays seemed to play over it constantly. When she went to bathe in the spring below her house, the rays of light surrounded her like a halo. The natives maintain that this bright light is still occasionally seen at Kahaiamano, indicating that the spirit of Kahalaopuna is revisiting her old home.

She was betrothed in childhood to Kauhi, the young chief of Kailua, in Koolau, whose parents were so sensible of the honor of the contemplated union of their son with the Princess of Manoa, who was deemed of a semi-supernatural descent, that they always sent the poi of Kailua and the fish of Kawainui for the girl's table. She was thus, as it were, brought up entirely on the food of her prospective husband.

When she was grown to young womanhood, she was so exquisitely beautiful that the people of the valley would make visits to the outer puloulou at the sacred precinct of Luaalea, the land adjoining Kahaiamano, just to get a glimpse of the beauty as she went to and from the spring. In this way the fame of her surpassing loveliness was spread all over the valley, and came to the ears of two men, Kumauna and Keawaa, both of whom were disfigured by a contraction of the lower eyelids, and were known as makahelei (drawn eyes). Neither of these men had ever seen Kahalaopuna, but they fell in love with her from hearsay, and not daring to present themselves to her as suitors on account of their disfigurement, they would weave and deck themselves in leis (wreaths) of maile (*Alyxia olivæ-formis*), ginger, and ferns and go to Waikiki for surf-bathing. While there they would indulge in boasting of their conquest of the famous beauty, representing the leis with which they were decked as love-gifts from Kahalaopuna. Now, when the surf of Kalehuawehe at Waikiki was in proper condition, it would attract people from all parts of the island to enjoy the delightful sport. Kauhi, the betrothed of Kahalaopuna, was one of these. The time set for his marriage to Kahalaopuna was drawing near, and as yet he had not seen her, when the assertions of the two makahelei men came to his ears. These were repeated so frequently that Kauhi finally came to believe them, and they so filled him with jealous rage of his betrothed that he determined to kill her. He started for Manoa at dawn, and proceeded as far as Mahinauli, in mid-valley, where he rested under a hala (*Pandanus odoratissimus*) tree that grew in the grove of wiliwili (*Erythrina monosperma*). He sat there some time, brooding over the fancied injury to himself, and nursing his wrath. Upon resuming his walk he broke off and carried along with him a bunch of hala nuts. It was quite noon when he reached Kahaiamano and presented himself before the house of Kahalaopuna. The latter had just awakened from a sleep, and was lying on a pile of mats facing the door, thinking of going to the spring, her usual bathing-place, when she perceived a stranger at the door.

She looked at him some time and, recognizing him from oft repeated descriptions, asked him to enter; but Kauhi refused, and asked her to come outside. The young girl had been so accustomed from early childhood to consider herself as belonging to Kauhi, and of being indebted to him, as it were, for her daily food, that she obeyed him unhesitatingly.

He perhaps intended to kill her then, but the girl's unhesitating obedience as well as her extreme loveliness made him hesitate for a while; and after looking intently at her for some time he told her to go and bathe and then prepare herself to accompany him in a ramble about the woods.

While Kahalaopuna was bathing, Kauhi remained moodily seated where she had left him, and watched the bright glow, like rainbow rays, playing above the spring. He was alternately filled with jealousy, regret, and longing for the great beauty of the girl; but that did not make him relent in his dreadful purpose. He seemed to resent his betrothed's supposed infidelity the more because she had thrown herself away on such unworthy persons, who were, besides, ugly and disfigured, while he, Kauhi, was not only a person of rank and distinction, but possessed also of considerable manly beauty.

When she was ready he motioned her to follow him, and turned to go without a word. They went across Kumakaha to Hualea, when the girl said, "Why don't you stay and have something to eat before we go?"

He answered rather surlily, "I don't care to eat; I have no appetite."

He looked so sternly at her as he said this that she cried out to him, "Are you annoyed with me? Have I displeased you in any way?"

He only said, "Why, what have you done that would displease me?"

He kept on his way, she following, till they came to a large stone in Aihualama, when he turned abruptly and, facing the young girl, looked at her with an expression of mingled longing and hate. At last, with a deep sigh, he said, "You are beautiful, my betrothed, but, as you have been false, you must die."

The young girl looked up in surprise at these strange words, but saw only hatred and a deadly purpose in Kauhi's eyes; so she said: "If I have to die, why did you not kill me at home, so that my people could have buried my bones; but you brought me to the wild woods, and who will bury me? If you think I have been false to you, why not seek proof before believing it?"

But Kauhi would not listen to her appeal. Perhaps it only served to remind him of what he considered was his great loss. He struck her across the temple with the heavy bunch of hala nuts he had broken off at Mahinauli, and which he had been holding all the time. The blow killed the girl instantly, and Kauhi hastily dug a hole under the side of the rock and buried her; then he started down the valley toward Waikiki.

As soon as he was gone, a large owl, who was a god, and a relative of Kahalaopuna, and had followed her from home, immediately set to digging the body out; which done, it brushed the dirt carefully off with its wings and, breathing into the girl's nostrils, restored her to life. It rubbed its face against the bruise on the temple, and healed it immediately. Kauhi had not advanced very far on his way when he heard the voice of Kahalaopuna singing a lament for his unkindness, and beseeching him to believe her, or, at least, prove his accusation.

Hearing her voice, Kauhi returned, and, seeing the owl flying above her, recognized the means of her resurrection; and, going up to the girl, ordered her to follow him. They went up the side of the ridge which divides Manoa Valley from Nuuanu. It was hard work for the tenderly nurtured maiden to climb the steep mountain ridge, at one time through a thorny tangle of underbrush, and at another clinging against the bare face of the rocks, holding on to swinging vines for support. Kauhi never offered to assist her, but kept on ahead, only looking back occasionally to see that she followed. When they arrived at the summit of the divide she was all scratched and bruised, her pa-u (skirt) in tatters. Seating herself on a stone to regain her breath, she asked Kauhi where they were going. He never answered, but struck her again with the hala branch, killing her instantly, as before. He then dug a hole near where she lay, and buried her, and started for Waikiki by way of the Kakea ridge. He was no sooner out of sight than the owl again scratched the dirt away and restored the girl, as before. Again she followed and sang a song of love and regret for her lover's anger, and pleaded with him to lay aside his unjust suspicions. On hearing her voice again, Kauhi returned and ordered her to follow him. They descended into Nuuanu Valley, at Kaniakapupu, and crossed over to Waolani ridge, where he again killed and buried the faithful girl, who was again restored by the owl. When he was on his way back, as before, she sang a song, describing the perils and difficulties of the way traversed by them, and ended by pleading for pardon for the unknown fault. The wretched man, on hearing her voice again, was very angry; and his repeated acts of cruelty and the suffering endured by the girl, far from softening his heart, only served to render him more brutal, and to extinguish what little spark of kindly feeling he might have had originally. His only thought was to kill her for good, and thus obtain some satisfaction for his wasted poi and fish. He returned to her and ordered her, as before, to follow him, and started for Kilohana, at the head of Kalihi Valley, where he again killed her. She was again restored by the owl, and made her resurrection known by singing to her cruel lover. He this time took her across gulches, ravines, and plains, until they arrived at Pohakea, on the Ewa slope of the Kaala Mountains, where he killed her and buried her under a large koa (*Acacia koa*) tree. The faithful owl tried to scrape the dirt away, so as to get at the body of the girl, but his claws became entangled in the numerous roots and rootlets which Kauhi had been careful not to cut away. The more the owl scratched, the more deeply tangled he got, and, finally, with bruised claws and ruffled feathers, he had to give up the idea of rescuing the girl; and perhaps he thought it useless, as she would be sure to make her resurrection known to Kauhi. So the owl left, and followed Kauhi on his return to Waikiki.

There had been another witness to Kauhi's cruelties, and that was Elepaio (*Chasiempis sandwichensis*), a little green bird, a cousin to Kahalaopuna. As soon as this bird saw that the owl had deserted the body of Kahalaopuna, it flew straight to Kahaukani and Kauakuahine, and told them of all that had happened. The girl had been missed, but, as some of the servants had recognized Kauhi, and had seen them leave together for what they supposed was a ramble in the adjoining woods, no great anxiety had been felt, as yet. But when the little bird told his tale, there was great consternation, and even positive disbelief; for, how could any one in his senses, they argued, be guilty of such, cruelty to such a lovely, innocent being, and one, too, belonging entirely to himself.

In the meantime, the spirit of the murdered girl discovered itself to a party who were passing by; and one of them, a young man, moved with compassion, went to the tree indicated by the spirit, and, removing the dirt and roots, found the body, still warm. He wrapped it in his kihei (shoulder scarf), and then covered it entirely with maile, ferns, and ginger, and, making a haawe, or back-load, of it, carried it to his home at Kamoiliili. There, he submitted the body to his elder brother, who called upon two spirit sisters of theirs, with whose aid they finally succeeded in restoring it to life. In the course of the treatment she was frequently taken to an underground water-cave, called Mauoki, for the Kakelekele (hydropathic cure). The water-cave has ever since been known as the "Water of Kahalaopuna."

The young man who had rescued her from the grave naturally wanted her to become his bride; but the girl refused, saying that as long as Kauhi lived she was his, and none other's, as her very body was, as it were, nourished on his food, and was as much his property as the food had been.

The elder brother then counselled the younger to seek, in some way, the death of Kauhi. To this end they conspired with the parents of Kahalaopuna to keep her last resurrection secret. The young man then set to work to learn all the meles Kahalaopuna had sung to her lover during that fatal journey. When he knew these songs well, he sought the kilu (play, or game) houses of the King and high chiefs, where Kauhi was sure to be found.

One day, when Kauhi was playing, this young man placed himself on the opposite side, and as Kauhi ceased, took up the kilu and chanted the first of Kahalaopuna's meles.

Kauhi was very much surprised, and contrary to the etiquette of the game of kilu, stopped him in his play to ask him where he had learned that song. The young man answered he had learned it from Kahalaopuna, the famous Manoa beauty, who was a friend of his sister's and who was now on a visit at their house. Kauhi, knowing the owl had deserted the body of the girl, felt certain that she was really dead, and accused the other of telling a lie. This led to an angry and stormy scene, when the antagonists were parted by orders of the King.

The next night found them both at the kilu house, when the second of Kahalaopuna's songs was sung, and another angry discussion took place. Again they were separated by others. On the third night, the third song having been sung, the dispute between the young men became so violent that Kauhi told the young man that the Kahalaopuna he knew must be an impostor, as the real person of that name was dead, to his certain knowledge. He dared him to produce the young woman whom he had been representing as Kahalaopuna; and should she not prove to be the genuine one then his life should be the forfeit, and on the other hand, if it should be the real one, then he, Kauhi, should be declared the liar and pay for his insults to the other with his life.

This was just what the young man had been scheming to compass, and he quickly assented to the challenge, calling on the King and chiefs to take notice of the terms of agreement, and to see that they were enforced.

On the appointed day Kahalaopuna went to Waikiki, attended by her parents, relatives, servants, and the two spirit sisters, who had assumed human form for that day so as to accompany their friend and advise her in case of necessity. Akaaka, the grandfather, who had been residing in Waikiki some little time previous to the dispute between the young men, was appointed one of the judges at the approaching trial.

Kauhi had consulted the priests and sorcerers of his family as to the possibility of the murdered girl having assumed human shape for the purpose of working him some injury. Kaea, a famous priest and seer of his family, told him to have the large leaves of the a-pe (*Calladium costatum*) spread where Kahalaopuna and party were to be seated. If she was a spirit, she would not be able to tear the a-pe leaf on which she would be seated, but if human, the leaf or leaves would be torn. With the permission of the King, this was done. The latter, surrounded by the highest chiefs and a vast assemblage from all parts of the island, was there to witness the test.

When Kahalaopuna and party were on the road to the scene of the test, her spirit friends informed her of the a-pe leaves, and advised her to trample on them so as to tear them as much as possible, as they, being spirits, would be unable to tear the leaves on which they should be seated, and if any one's attention were drawn to them, they would be found out and killed by the poe po-i uhane (spirit catchers).

The young girl faithfully performed what was required of her. Kaea, on seeing the torn leaves, remarked that she was evidently human, but that he felt the presence of spirits, and would watch for them, feeling sure they were in some way connected with the girl. Akaaka then told him to look in a calabash of water, when he would in all probability see the spirits. The seer, in his eagerness to unravel the mystery, forgot his usual caution and ordered a vessel of water to be brought, and, looking in, he saw only his own reflection. Akaaka at that moment caught the reflection of the seer (which was his spirit), and crushed it between his palms, and at that moment the seer dropped down dead. Akaaka now turned around and opened his arms and embraced Kahalaopuna, thus acknowledging her as his own beloved granddaughter.

The King now demanded of the girl and of Kauhi an account of all that had happened between them, and of the reported death of the maiden. They both told their stories, Kauhi ascribing his anger to hearing the assertions of the two disfigured men, Kumauna and Keawaa. These two, on being confronted with the girl, acknowledged never having seen her before, and that all their words had been idle boastings. The King then said: "As your fun has cost this innocent girl so much suffering, it is my will that you two and Kauhi suffer death at once, as a matter of justice; and if your gods are powerful enough to restore you, so much the better for you."

Two large imus (ground ovens) had been heated by the followers of the young men, in anticipation of the possible fate of either, and Kauhi, with the two mischief-makers and such of their respective followers and retainers as preferred to die with their chiefs, were baked therein.

The greater number of Kauhi's people were so incensed with his cruelty to the lovely young girl that they transferred their allegiance to her, offering themselves for her vassals as restitution, in a measure, for the undeserved sufferings borne by her at the hands of their cruel chief.

The King gave her for a bride to the young man who had not only saved her, but had been the means of avenging her wrongs.

The imus in which Kauhi and his companions were baked were on the side of the stream of Apuakehau, in the famous Ulukou grove, and very near the sea. The night following, a great tidal wave, sent in by a powerful old shark god, a relative of Kauhi's, swept over the site of the two ovens, and in the morning it was seen that their contents had disappeared. The bones had been taken by the old shark into the sea. The chiefs, Kumauna and Keawaa, were, through the power of their family gods, transformed into the two mountain peaks on the eastern corner of Manoa Valley, while Kauhi and his followers were turned into sharks.

Kahalaopuna lived happily with her husband for about two years. Her grandfather, knowing of Kauhi's transformation, and aware of his vindictive nature, strictly forbade her from ever going into the sea. She remembered and heeded the warning during those years, but one day, her husband and all their men having gone to Manoa to cultivate kalo (*Colocasia antiquorum*), she was left alone with her maid servants.

The surf on that day was in fine sporting condition, and a number of young women were surf-riding, and Kahalaopuna longed to be with them. Forgetting the warning, as soon as her mother fell asleep she slipped out with one of her maids and swam out on a surf-board. This was Kauhi's opportunity, and as soon as she was fairly outside the reef he bit her in two and held the upper half of the body up out of the water, so that all the surf-bathers would see and know that he had at last obtained his revenge.

Immediately on her death the spirit of the young woman went back and told her sleeping mother of what had befallen her. The latter woke up, and, missing her, gave the alarm. This was soon confirmed by the terrified surf-bathers, who had all fled ashore at seeing the terrible fate of Kahalaopuna. Canoes were launched and manned, and chase given to the shark and his prey, which could be easily tracked by the blood.

He swam just far enough below the surface of the water to be visible, and yet too far to be reached with effect by the fishing-spears of the pursuers. He led them a long chase to Waianae; then, in a sandy opening in the bottom of the sea, where everything was visible to the pursuers, he ate up the young woman, so that she could never again be restored to this life.

Her parents, on hearing of her end, retired to Manoa Valley, and gave up their human life, resolving themselves into their supernatural elements. Kahaukani, the father, is known as the Manoa wind, but his usual and visible form is the grove of ha-u (hibiscus) trees, below Kahaiamano. Kauakuahine, the mother, assumed her rain form, and is very often to be met with about the former home of her beloved child.

The grandparents also gave up their human forms, and returned, the one to his mountain form, and the other into the lehua bushes still to be met with on the very brow of the hill, where they keep watch over the old home of their petted and adored grandchild.

THE MERMAID'S VENGEANCE

Cornwall

In one of the deep valleys of the parish of Perranzabuloe, which are remarkable for their fertility, and especially for the abundance of fruit which the orchards produce, lived in days long ago, amidst a rudely-civilised people, a farmer's labourer, his wife, with one child, a daughter. The man and woman were equally industrious. The neatly white-washed walls of their mud-built cottage, the well-kept gravelled paths, and carefully-weeded beds of their small garden, in which flowers were cultivated for ornament, and vegetables for use, proclaimed at once the character of the inmates. In contrast with the neighbouring cottages, this one, although smaller than many others, had a superior aspect, and the occupiers of it exhibited a strong contrast to those peasants and miners amidst whom they dwelt.

Pennaluna, as the man was called, or Penna the Proud, as he was, in no very friendly spirit, named by his less thoughtful and more impulsive fellows, was, as we have said, a farmer's labourer. His master was a wealthy yeoman, and he, after many years' experience, was so convinced of the exceeding industry and sterling honesty of Penna, that he made him the manager of an outlying farm in this parish, under the hind (or hine—the Saxon pronunciation is still retained in the West of England), or general supervisor of this and numerous other extensive farms.

Penna was too great a favourite with the Squire to be a favourite of the hind's; he was evidently jealous of him, and from not being himself a man of very strict principles, he hated the unobtrusive goodness of his underling, and was constantly on the watch to discover some cause of complaint. It was not, however, often that he was successful in this. Every task committed to the care of Penna,—and he was often purposely overtasked,—was executed with great care and despatch. With the wife of Penna, however, the case was unfortunately different. Honour Penna was as industrious as her husband, and to him she was in all respects a helpmate. She had, however, naturally a proud spirit, and this had been encouraged in her youth by her parents. Honour was very pretty as a girl, and, indeed, she retained much beauty as a woman. The only education she received was the wild one of experience, and this within a very narrow circle. She grew an ignorant girl, amongst ignorant men and women, few of them being able to write their names, and scarcely any of them to read. There was much native grace about her, and she was flattered by the young men, and envied by the young women, of the village—the envy and the flattery being equally pleasant to her. In the same village was born, and brought up, Tom Chenalls, who had, in the course of years, become hind to the Squire. Tom, as a young man, had often expressed himself fond of Honour, but he was always distasteful to the village maiden, and eventually, while yet young, she was married to Pennaluna, who came from the southern coast, bringing with him the recommendation of being a stranger, and an exceedingly hard-working man, who was certain to earn bread, and something more, for his wife and family. In the relations in which these people were now placed towards each other, Chenalls had the opportunity of acting ungenerously towards the Pennas. The man bore this uncomplainingly, but the woman frequently quarrelled with him whom she felt was an enemy, and whom she still regarded but as her equal. Chenalls was a skilled farmer, and hence was of considerable value to the Squire; but although he was endured for his farming knowledge and his business habits, he was never a favourite with his employer. Penna, on the contrary, was an especial favourite, and the evidences of this were so often brought strikingly under the observation of Chenalls, that it increased the irritation of his hate, for it amounted to that. For years things went on thus. There was the tranquil suffering of an oppressed spirit manifested in Penna—the angry words and actions of his wife towards the oppressor,—and, at the same time, as she with much fondness studied to make their humble home comfortable for her husband, she reviled him not unfrequently for the meek spirit with which he endured his petty, but still trying, wrongs. The hind dared not venture on any positive act of wrong towards those people, yet he lost no chance of annoying them, knowing that the Squire's partiality for Penna would not allow him to venture beyond certain bounds, even in this direction.

Penna's solace was his daughter. She had now reached her eighteenth year, and with the well-developed form of a woman, she united the simplicity of a child. Selina, as she was named, was in many respects beautiful. Her features were regular, and had they been lighted up with more mental fire, they would have been beautiful; but the constant repose, the want of animation, left her face merely a pretty one. Her skin was beautifully white, and transparent to the blue veins which traced their ways beneath it, to the verge of that delicacy which indicates disease; but it did not pass that verge. Selina was full of health, as her well moulded form at once showed, and her clear blue eye distinctly told. At times there was a lovely tint upon the cheek—not the hectic of consumptive beauty,—but a pure rosy dye, suffused by the healthy life stream, when it flowed the fastest.

The village gossips, who were always busy with their neighbours, said strange things of this girl. Indeed, it was commonly reported that the real child of the Pennas was a remarkably plain child, in every respect a different being from Selina. The striking difference between the infant and the woman was variously explained by the knowing ones. Two stories were, however, current for miles around the country. One was, that Selina's mother was constantly seen gathering dew in the morning, with which to wash her child, and that the fairies on the Towens had, in pure malice, aided her in giving a temporary beauty to the girl, that it might lead to her betrayal into crime. Why this malice, was never clearly made out.

The other story was, that Honour Penna constantly bathed the child in a certain pool, amidst the arched rocks of Perran, which was a favourite resort of the mermaids; that on one occasion the child, as if in a paroxysm of joy, leapt from her arms into the water, and disappeared. The mother, as may well be supposed, suffered a momentary agony of terror; but presently the babe swam up to the surface of the water, its little face more bright and beautiful than it had ever been before. Great was the mother's joy, and also—as the gossips say—great her surprise at the sudden change in the appearance of her offspring. The mother knew no difference in the child whom she pressed lovingly to her bosom, but all the aged crones in the parish declared it to be a changeling. This tale lived its day; but, as the girl grew on to womanhood, and showed none of the special qualifications belonging either to fairies or mermaids, it was almost forgotten. The uncomplaining father had solace for all his sufferings in wandering over the beautiful sands with his daughter. Whether it was when the summer seas fell in musical undulations on the shore, or when, stirred by the winter tempests, the great Atlantic waves came up in grandeur, and lashed the resisting sands in giant rage, those two enjoyed the solitude. Hour after hour, from the setting sun time, until the clear cold moon flooded the ocean with her smiles of light, would the father and child walk these sands. They seemed never to weary of them and the ocean.

Almost every morning, throughout the milder seasons, Selina was in the habit of bathing, and wild tales were told of the frantic joy with which she would play with the breaking billows. Sometimes floating over, and almost dancing on the crests of the waves, at other times rushing under them, and allowing the breaking waters to beat her to the sands, as though they were loving arms, endeavouring to encircle her form. Certain it is, that Selina greatly enjoyed her bath, but all the rest must be regarded as the creations of the imagination. The most eager to give a construction unfavourable to the simple mortality of the maiden was, however, compelled to acknowledge that there was no evidence in her general conduct to support their surmises. Selina, as an only child, fared the fate of others who are unfortunately so placed, and was, as the phrase is, spoiled. She certainly was allowed to follow her own inclinations without any check. Still her inclinations were bounded to working in the garden, and to leading her father to the sea-shore. Honour Penna, sometimes, it is true, did complain that Selina could not be trusted with the most ordinary domestic duty. Beyond this, there was one other cause of grief, that was, the increasing dislike which Selina exhibited towards entering a church. The girl, notwithstanding the constant excuses of being sick, suffering from headache, having a pain in her side, and the like, was often taken, notwithstanding, by her mother to the church. It is said that she always shuddered as she passed the church-stile, and again on stepping from the porch into the church itself. When once within the house of prayer she evinced no peculiar liking or disliking, observing respectfully all the rules during the performance of the church-service, and generally sleeping, or seeming to sleep, during the sermon. Selina Pennaluna had reached her eighteenth year; she was admired by many of the young men of the parish, but, as if surrounded by a spell, she appeared to keep them all at a distance from her. About this time, a nephew to the Squire, a young soldier—who had been wounded in the wars—came into Cornwall to heal his wounds, and recover health, which had suffered in a trying campaign.

This young man, Walter Trewoofe, was a rare specimen of manhood. Even now, shattered as he was by the combined influences of wounds, an unhealthy climate, and dissipation, he could not but be admired for fineness of form, dignity of carriage, and masculine beauty. It was, however, but too evident, that this young man was his own idol, and that he expected every one to bow down with him, and worship it. His uncle was proud of Walter, and although the old gentleman could not fail to see many faults, yet he regarded them as the follies of youth, and trusted to their correction with the increase of years and experience. Walter, who was really suffering severely, was ordered by his surgeon, at first, to take short walks on the sea-shore, and, as he gained strength, to bathe. He was usually driven in his uncle's pony-carriage to the edge of the sands. Then dismounting he would walk for a short time, and quickly wearing, return in his carriage to the luxuriant couches at the manor-house.

On some of those occasions Walter had observed the father and daughter taking their solitary ramble. He was struck with the quiet beauty of the girl, and seized an early opportunity of stopping Penna to make some general inquiry respecting the bold and beautiful coast. From time to time they thus met, and it would have been evident to any observer that Walter did not so soon weary of the sands as formerly, and that Selina was not displeased with the flattering things he said to her. Although the young soldier had hitherto led a wild life, it would appear as if for a considerable period the presence of goodness had repressed every tendency to evil in his ill-regulated heart. He continued, therefore, for some time playing with his own feelings and those of the childlike being who presented so much of romance, combined with the most homely tameness, of character. Selina, it is true, had never yet seen Walter except in the presence of her father, and it is questionable if she had ever for one moment had a warmer feeling than that of the mere pleasure—a silent pride—that a gentleman, at once so handsome, so refined, and the nephew of her father's master, should pay her any attention. Evil eyes were watching with wicked earnestness the growth of passion, and designing hearts were beating quicker with a consciousness that they should eventually rejoice in the downfall of innocence. Tom Chenalls hoped that he might achieve a triumph, if he could but once asperse the character of Selina. He took his measures accordingly. Having noticed the change in the general conduct of his master's nephew, he argued that this was due to the refining influence of a pure mind, acting on one more than ordinarily impressionable to either evil or good.

Walter rapidly recovered health, and with renewed strength the manly energy of his character began to develop itself. He delighted in horse-exercise, and Chenalls had always the best horse on the farms at his disposal. He was a good shot, and Chenalls was his guide to the best shooting-grounds. He sometimes fished, and Chenalls knew exactly where the choicest trout and the richest salmon were to be found. In fact, Chenalls entered so fully into the tastes of the young man, that Walter found him absolutely necessary to him to secure the enjoyments of a country life.

Having established this close intimacy, Chenalls never lost an opportunity of talking with Walter respecting Selina Penna. He soon satisfied himself that Walter, like most other young men who had led a dissipated life, had but a very low estimate of women generally. Acting upon this, he at first insinuated that Selina's innocence was but a mask, and at length he boldly assured Walter that the cottage girl was to be won by him with a few words, and that then he might put her aside at any time as a prize to some low-born peasant. Chenalls never failed to impress on Walter the necessity of keeping his uncle in the most perfect darkness, and of blinding the eyes of Selina's parents. Penna was,—so thought Chenalls,— easily managed, but there was more to be feared from the wife. Walter, however, with much artifice, having introduced himself to Honour Penna, employed the magic of that flattery, which, being properly applied, seldom fails to work its way to the heart of a weak-minded woman. He became an especial favourite with Honour, and the blinded mother was ever pleased at the attention bestowed with so little assumption—as she thought—of pride, on her daughter, by one so much above them. Walter eventually succeeded in separating occasionally, though not often, Penna and his daughter. The witching whispers of unholy love were poured into the trusting ear. Guileless herself, this child-woman suspected no guile in others, least of all in one whom she had been taught to look upon as a superior being to herself. Amongst the villagers, the constant attention of Walter Trewoofe was the subject of gossip, and many an old proverb was quoted by the elder women, ill-naturedly, and implying that evil must come of this intimacy, Tom Chenalls was now employed by Walter to contrive some means by which he could remove Penna for a period from home. He was not long in doing this. He lent every power of his wicked nature to aid the evil designs of the young soldier, and thus he brought about that separation of father and child which ended in her ruin.

Near the Land's End the squire possessed some farms, and one of them was reported to be in such a state of extreme neglect, through the drunkenness and consequent idleness of the tenant, that Chenalls soon obtained permission to take the farm from this occupier, which he did in the most unscrupulous disregard for law or right. It was then suggested that the only plan by which a desirable occupier could be found, would be to get the farm and farm-buildings into good condition, and that Penna, of all men, would be the man to bring this quickly about. The squire was pleased with the plan. Penna was sent for by him, and was proud of the confidence which his master reposed in him. There was some sorrow on his leaving home. He subsequently said that he had had many warnings not to go, but he felt that he dared not disoblige a master who had trusted him so far—so he went.

Walter needed not any urging on the part of Chenalls, though he was always ready to apply the spur when there was the least evidence of the sense of right asserting itself in the young man's bosom. Week after week passed on. Walter had rendered himself a necessity to Selina. Without her admirer the world was cold and colourless. With him all was sunshine and glowing tints.

Three months passed thus away, and during that period it had only been possible for Penna to visit his home twice. The father felt that something like a spirit of evil stood between him and his daughter. There was no outward evidence of any change, but there was an inward sense—undefined, yet deeply felt—like an overpowering fear—that some wrong had been done. On parting, Penna silently but earnestly prayed that the deep dread might be removed from his mind. There was an aged fisherman, who resided in a small cottage built on the sands, who possessed all the superstitions of his class. This old man had formed a father's liking for the simple-hearted maiden, and he had persuaded himself that there really was some foundation for the tales which the gossips told. To the fisherman, Walter Trewoofe was an evil genius. He declared that no good ever came to him, if he met Walter when he was about to go to sea. With this feeling he curiously watched the young man and maiden, and he, in after days, stated his conviction that he had seen "merry maidens rising from the depth of the waters, and floating under the billows to watch Selina and her lover. He has also been heard to say that on more than one occasion Walter himself had been terrified by sights and sounds. Certain, however, it is, these were insufficient and the might of evil passions were more powerful than any of the protecting influences of the unseen world.

Another three months had gone by, and Walter Trewoofe had disappeared from Perranzabuloe. He had launched into the gay world of the metropolis, and rarely, if ever, dreamed of the deep sorrow which was weighing down the heart he had betrayed. Penna returned home—his task was done—and Chenalls had no reason for keeping him any longer from his wife and daughter. Clouds gathered slowly but unremittingly around him. His daughter retired into herself no longer as of old reposing her whole soul on her father's heart. His wife was somewhat changed too—she had some secret in her heart which she feared to tell. The home he had left was not the home to which he had returned. It soon became evident that some shock had shaken the delicate frame of his daughter. She pined rapidly; and Penna was awakened to a knowledge of the cause by the rude rejoicing of Chenalls, who declared "that all people who kept themselves so much above other people were sure to be pulled down." On one occasion he so far tempted Penna with sneers, at his having hope to secure the young squire for a son-in-law, that the long-enduring man broke forth and administered a severe blow upon his tormentor. This was duly reported to the squire, and added thereto was a magnified story of a trap which had been set by the Penna to catch young Walter; it was represented that even now they intended to press their claims, on account of grievous wrongs upon them, whereas it could be proved that Walter was guiltless—that he was indeed the innocent victim of designing people, who thought to make money out of their assumed misfortune. The squire made his inquiries, and there were not a few who eagerly seized the opportunity to gain the friendship of Chenalls by representing this family to have been hypocrites of the deepest dye; and the poor girl especially was now loaded with a weight of iniquities of which she had no knowledge. All this ended in the dismissal of Penna from the Squire's service, and in his being deprived of the cottage in which he had taken so much pride. Although thrown out upon the world a disgraced man, Penna faced his difficulties manfully. He cast off, as it were, the primitive simplicity of his character, and evidently worked with a firm resolve to beat down his sorrows. He was too good a workman to remain long unemployed; and although his new home was not his happy home as of old, there was no repining heard from his lips. Weaker and weaker grew Selina, and it soon became evident to all, that if she came from a spirit-world, to a spirit-world she must soon return. Grief filled the hearts of her parents—it prostrated her mother, but the effects of severe labour, and the efforts of a settled mind, appeared to tranquillise the breast of her father. Time passed on, the wounds of the soul grew deeper, and there lay, on a low bed, from which she had not strength to move, the fragile form of youth with the countenance of age. The body was almost powerless, but there beamed from the eye the evidences of a spirit getting free from the chains of clay.

The dying girl was sensible of the presence of creations other than mortal, and with these she appeared to hold converse, and to derive solace from the communion. Penna and his wife alternately watched through the night hours by the side of their loved child, and anxiously did they mark the moment when the tide turned, in the full belief that she would be taken from them when the waters of the ocean began to recede from the shore. Thus days passed on, and eventually the sunlight of a summer morning shone in through the small window of this humble cottage,—on a dead mother—and a living babe.

The dead was buried in the churchyard on the sands, and the living went on their ways, some rejoicingly and some in sorrow.

Once more Walter Trewoofe appeared in Perran-on-the-sands. Penna would have sacrificed him to his hatred; he emphatically protested that he had lived only to do so; but the good priest of the Oratory contrived to lay the devil who had possession, and to convince Penna that the Lord would, in His own good time, and in His own way, avenge the bitter wrong. Tom Chenalls had his hour of triumph; but from the day on which Selina died everything went wrong. The crops failed, the cattle died, hay-stacks and corn-ricks caught fire, cows slipped their calves, horses fell lame, or stumbled and broke their knees—a succession of evils steadily pursued him. Trials find but a short resting-place with the good; they may be bowed to the earth with the weight of a sudden sorrow, but they look to heaven, and their elasticity is restored. The evil-minded are crushed at once, and grovel on the ground in irremediable misery. That Chenalls fled to drink in his troubles appeared but the natural result to a man of his character. This unfitted him for his duties, and he was eventually dismissed from his situation. Notwithstanding that the Squire refused to listen to the appeals in favour of Chenalls, which were urged upon him by Walter, and that indeed he forbade his nephew to countenance "the scoundrel" in any way, Walter still continued his friend. By his means Tom Chenalls secured a small cottage on the cliff, and around it a little cultivated ground, the produce of which was his only visible means of support. That lonely cottage was the scene, however, of drunken carousals, and there the vicious young men, and the no less vicious young women, of the district, went after nightfall, and kept "high carnival" of sin. Walter Trewoofe came frequently amongst them; and as his purse usually defrayed the costs of a debauch, he was regarded by all with especial favour.

One midnight, Walter, who had been dancing and drinking for some hours, left the cottage wearied with his excesses, and although not drunk, he was much excited with wine. His pathway lay along the edge of the cliffs, amidst bushes of furze and heath, and through several irregular, zigzag ways. There were lateral paths striking off from one side of the main path, and leading down to the sea-shore. Although it was moonlight, without being actually aware of the error, Walter wandered into one of those; and before he was awake to his mistake, he found himself on the sands. He cursed his stupidity, and, uttering a blasphemous oath, he turned to retrace his steps.

The most exquisite music which ever flowed from human lips fell on his ear; he paused to listen, and collecting his unbalanced thoughts, he discovered that it was the voice of a woman singing a melancholy dirge:—

"The stars are beautiful, when bright
They are mirror'd in the sea;
But they are pale beside that light
Which was so beautiful to me.
My angel child, my earth-born girl,
From all your kindred riven,
By the base deeds of a selfish churl,
And to a sand-grave driven!
How shall I win thee back to ocean?
How canst thou quit thy grave,
To share again the sweet emotion
Of gliding through the wave?"

Walter, led by the melancholy song, advanced slowly along the sands. He discovered that the sweet, soft sounds proceeded from the other side of a mass of rocks, which project far out over the sands, and that now, at low-water, there was no difficulty in walking around it. Without hesitation he did so, and he beheld, sitting at the mouth of a cavern, one of the most beautiful women he had ever beheld. She continued her song, looking upwards to the stars, not appearing to notice the intrusion of a stranger. Walter stopped, and gazed on the lovely image before him with admiration and wonder, mingled with something of terror. He dared not speak, but fixed, as if by magic, he stood gazing on. After a few minutes, the maiden, suddenly perceiving that a man was near her, uttered a piercing shriek, and made as if to fly into the cavern. Walter sprang forward and seized her by the arm, exclaiming, "Not yet, my pretty maiden, not yet."

She stood still in the position of flight, with her arm behind her, grasped by Walter, and turning round her head, her dark eyes beamed with unnatural lustre upon him. Impressionable he had ever been, but never had he experienced anything so entrancing, and at the same time so painful, as that gaze. It was Selina's face looking lovingly upon him, but it seemed to possess some new power—a might of mind from which he felt it was impossible for him to escape. Walter slackened his hold, and slowly allowed the arm to fall from his hand. The maiden turned fully round upon him. "Go!" she said. He could not move. "Go, man!" she repeated. He was powerless.

"Go to the grave where the sinless one sleepeth!
Bring her cold corse where her guarding one weepeth;
Look on her, love her again, ay! betray her,
And wreath with false smiles the pale face of her slayer!
Go, go! now, and feel the full force of my sorrow!
For the glut of my vengeance there cometh a morrow."

Walter was statue-like, and he awoke from this trance-like state only when the waves washed his feet, and he became aware that even now it was only by wading through the waters that he could return around the point of rocks. He was alone. He called; no one answered. He sought wildly, as far as he now dared, amidst the rocks, but the lovely woman was nowhere to be discovered.

There was no real danger on such a night as this; therefore Walter walked fearlessly through the gentle waves, and recovered the pathway up from the sands. More than once he thought he heard a rejoicing laugh, which was echoed in the rocks, but no one was to be seen. Walter reached his home and bed, but he found no sleep; and in the morning he arose with a sense of wretchedness which was entirely new to him. He feared to make any one of his rough companions a confidant, although he felt this would have relieved his heart. He therefore nursed the wound which he now felt, until a bitter remorse clouded his existence. After some days, he was impelled to visit the grave of the lost one, and in the fullness of the most selfish sorrow, he sat on the sands and shed tears. The priest of the Oratory observed him, and knowing Walter Trewoofe, hesitated not to inquire into his cause of sorrow. His heart was opened to the holy man, and the strange tale was told—the only result being, that the priest felt satisfied it was but a vivid dream, which had resulted from a brain over-excited by drink. He, however, counselled the young man, giving him some religious instruction, and dismissed him with his blessing. There was relief in this. For some days Walter did not venture to visit his old haunt, the cottage of Chenalls. Since he could not be lost to his companions without greatly curtailing their vicious enjoyments, he was hunted up by Chenalls, and again enticed within the circle. His absence was explained on the plea of illness. Walter was, however, an altered man; there was not the same boisterous hilarity as formerly. He no longer abandoned himself without restraint to the enjoyments of the time. If he ever, led on by his thoughtless and rough-natured friends, assumed for a moment his usual mirth, it was checked by some invisible power. On such occasions he would turn deadly pale, look anxiously around, and fall back, as if ready to faint, on the nearest seat. Under these influences, he lost health. His uncle, who was really attached to his nephew, although he regretted his dissolute conduct, became now seriously alarmed. Physicians were consulted in vain; the young man pined, and the old gossips came to the conclusion that Walter Trewoofe was ill-wished, and there was a general feeling that Penna or his wife was at the bottom of it. Walter, living really on one idea, and that one the beautiful face which was, and yet was not, that of Selina, resolved again to explore the spot on which he had met this strange being, of whom nothing could be learned by any of the covert inquiries he made. He lingered long ere he could resolve on the task; but wearied, worn by the oppression of one undefined idea, in which an intensity of love was mixed with a shuddering fear, he at last gathered sufficient courage to seize an opportunity for again going to the cavern. On this occasion, there being no moon, the night was dark, but the stars shone brightly from a sky, cloudless, save a dark mist which hung heavily over the western horizon. Every spot of ground being familiar to him, who, boy and man, had traced it over many times, the partial darkness presented no difficulty. Walter had scarcely reached the level sands, which were left hard by the retiring tide, than he heard again the same magical voice as before. But now the song was a joyous one, the burthen of it being—

"Join all hands—
Might and main,
Weave the sands,
Form a chain,

He, my lover,

Comes again!"

He could not entirely dissuade himself but that he heard this repeated by many voices; but he put the thought aside, referring it, as well he might, to the numerous echoes from the cavernous openings in the cliffs.

He reached the eastern side of the dark mass of rocks, from the point of which the tide was slowly subsiding. The song had ceased, and a low moaning sound—the soughing of the wind—passed along the shore. Walter trembled with fear, and was on the point of returning, when a most flute-like murmur rose from the other side of the rocky barrier, which was presently moulded into words—

"From your couch of glistering pearl,

Slowly, softly, come away;

Our sweet earth-child, lovely girl,

Died this day,—died this day."

Memory told Walter that truly was it the anniversary of Selina Pennaluna's death, and to him every gentle wave falling on the shore sang, or murmured—

"Died this day—died this day."

The sand was left dry around the point of the rocks, and Walter impelled by a power which he could not control, walked onward. The moment he appeared on the western side of the rock, a wild laugh burst into the air, as if from the deep cavern before him, at the entrance of which sat the same beautiful being whom he had formerly met. There was now an expression of rare joy on her face, her eyes glistened with delight, and she extended her arms. as if to welcome him.

"Was it ever your wont to move so slowly towards your loved one?"

Walter heard it was Selina's voice. He saw it was Selina's features; but he was conscious it was not Selina's form.

"Come, sit beside me, Walter, and let us talk of love." He sat down without a word, and looked into the maiden's face with a vacant expression of fondness. Presently she placed her hand upon his heart; a shudder passed through his frame; but having passed, he felt no more pain, but a rare intensity of delight. The maiden wreathed her arm around his neck, drew Walter towards her, and then he remembered how often he had acted thus towards Selina. She bent over him and looked into his eyes. In his mind's mirror he saw himself looking thus into the eyes of his betrayed one.

"You loved her once?" said the maiden.

"I did indeed," answered Walter, with a sigh.

"As you loved her, so I love you," said the maiden, with a smile which shot like a poisoned dart through Walter's heart. She lifted the young man's head lovingly between her hands, and bending over him, pressed her lips upon and kissed his forehead, Walter curiously felt that although he was the kissed, yet that he was the kisser.

"Kisses," she said, "are as true at sea as they are false on land. You men kiss the earth-born maidens to betray them. The kiss of a sea-child is the seal of constancy. You are mine till death."

"Death!" almost shrieked Walter.

A full consciousness of his situation now broke upon Walter. He had heard the tales of the gossips respecting the mermaid origin of Selina; but he had laughed at them as an idle fancy. he now felt they were true. For hours Walter was compelled to sit by the side of his beautiful tormentor, every word of assumed love and rapture being a torture of the most exquisite kind to him. He could not escape from the arms which were wound around him. He saw the tide rising rapidly. He heard the deep voice of the winds coming over the sea from the far west. He saw that which appeared at first as a dark mist, shape itself into a dense black mass of cloud, and rise rapidly over the star-bedecked space above him. He saw by the brilliant edge of light which occasionally fringed the clouds that they were deeply charged with thunder. There was something sublime in the steady motion of the storm; and now the roll of the waves, which had been disturbed in the Atlantic, reached our shores, and the breakers fell thunderingly within a few feet of Walter and his companion. Paroxysms of terror shook him, and with each convulsion he felt himself grasped with still more ardour, and pressed so closely to the maiden's bosom, that he heard her heart dancing of joy.

At length his terrors gave birth to words, and he implored her to let him go.

"The kiss of the sea-child is the seal of constancy." Walter vehemently implored forgiveness. He confessed his deep iniquity. He promised a life of penitence.

"Give me back the dead," said the maiden bitterly, and she planted another kiss, which seemed to pierce his brain by its coldness, upon his forehead.

The waves rolled around the rock on which they sat; they washed their seat. Walter was still in the female's grasp, and she lifted him to a higher ledge. The storm approached. Lightnings struck down from the heavens into the sands; and thunders roared along the iron cliffs. The mighty waves grew yet more rash, and washed up to this strange pair, who now sat on the highest pinnacle of the pile of rocks. Walter's terrors nearly overcame him; but he was roused by a liquid stream of fire, which positively hissed by him, followed immediately by a crash of thunder, which shook the solid earth. Tom Chenall's cottage on the cliff burst into a blaze, and Walter saw, from his place amidst the raging waters, a crowd of male and female roisterers rush terrified out upon the heath, to be driven back by the pelting storm. The climax of horrors appeared to surround Walter. He longed to end it in death, but he could not die. His senses were quickened. He saw his wicked companion and evil adviser struck to the ground, a blasted heap of ashes, by a lightning stroke, and at the same moment he and his companion were borne off the rock on the top of a mountainous wave, on which he floated; the woman holding him by the hair of his head, and singing in a rejoicing voice, which was like a silver bell heard amidst the deep base bellowings of the storm—

"Come away, come away,
O'er the waters wild!
Our earth-born child
Died this day, died this day.
"Come away, come away!
The tempest loud
Weaves the shroud
For him who did betray.
"Come away, come away!
Beneath the wave
Lieth the grave
Of him we slay, him we slay.

"Come away, come away!
He shall not rest
In earth's own breast
For many a day, many a day.
"Come away, come away!
By billows to
From coast to coast,
Like deserted boat
His corse shall float
Around the bay, around the bay."

Myriads of voices on that wretched night were heard amidst the roar of the storm. The waves were seen covered with a multitudinous host, who were tossing from one to the other the dying Walter Trewoofe, whose false heart thus endured the vengeance of the mermaid, who had, in the fondness of her soul, made the innocent child of humble parents the child of her adoption.

A STRANGE CATCH

THE MERMAN

Iceland

Long ago a farmer lived at Vogar, who was a mighty fisherman, and, of all the farms round about not one was so well situated with regard to the fisheries as his.

One day, according to custom, he had gone out fishing, and having cast down his line from the boat, and waited awhile, found it very hard to pull up again, as if there were something very heavy at the end of it. Imagine his astonishment when he found that what he had caught was a great fish, with a man's head and body! When he saw that this creature was alive, he addressed it and said, "Who and whence are you?"

"A merman from the bottom of the sea," was the reply.

The farmer then asked him what he had been doing when the hook caught his flesh.

The other replied, "I was turning the cowl of my mother's chimney-pot, to suit it to the wind. So let me go again, will you?"

"Not for the present," said the fisherman. "You shall serve me awhile first."

So without more words he dragged him into the boat and rowed to shore with him.

When they got to the boat-house, the fisherman's dog came to him and greeted him joyfully, barking and fawning on him, and wagging his tail. But his master's temper being none of the best, he struck the poor animal; whereupon the merman laughed for the first time.

Having fastened the boat, he went towards his house, dragging his prize with him, over the fields, and stumbling over a hillock, which lay in his way, cursed it heartily; whereupon the merman laughed for the second time.

When the fisherman arrived at the farm, his wife came out to receive him, and embraced him affectionately, and he received her salutations with pleasure; whereupon the merman laughed for the third time.

Then said the farmer to the merman, "You have laughed three times, and I am curious to know why you have laughed. Tell me, therefore."

"Never will I tell you," replied the merman, "unless you promise to take me to the same place in the sea wherefrom you caught me, and there to let me go free again." So the farmer made him the promise.

"Well," said the merman, "I laughed the first time because you struck your dog, whose joy at meeting you was real and sincere. The second time, because you cursed the mound over which you stumbled, which is full of golden ducats. And the third time, because you received with pleasure your wife's empty and flattering embrace, who is faithless to you, and a hypocrite. And now be an honest man and take me out to the sea whence you have brought me."

The farmer replied: "Two things that you have told me I have no means of proving, namely, the faithfulness of my dog and the faithlessness of my wife. But the third I will try the truth of, and if the hillock contain gold, then I will believe the rest."

Accordingly he went to the hillock, and having dug it up, found therein a great treasure of golden ducats, as the merman had told him. After this the farmer took the merman down to the boat, and to that place in the sea whence he had caught him. Before he put him in, the latter said to him:

"Farmer, you have been an honest man, and I will reward you for restoring me to my mother, if only you have skill enough to take possession of property that I shall throw in your way. Be happy and prosper."

Then the farmer put the merman into the sea, and he sank out of sight.

It happened that not long after, seven sea-grey cows were seen on the beach, close to the farmer's land. These cows appeared to be very unruly, and ran away directly the farmer approached them. So he took a stick and ran after them, possessed with the fancy that if he could burst the bladder which he saw on the nose of each of them, they would belong to him. He contrived to hit out the bladder on the nose of one cow, which then became so tame that he could easily catch it, while the others leaped into the sea and disappeared. The farmer was convinced that this was the gift of the merman. And a very useful gift it was, for better cow was never seen nor milked in all the land, and she was the mother of the race of grey cows so much esteemed now.

And the farmer prospered exceedingly, but never caught any more mermen. As for his wife, nothing further is told about her, so we can repeat nothing.

THE OLD MAN
WHO BECAME a FISH

Korea

Some years ago a noted official became the magistrate of Ko-song County. On a certain day a guest called on him to pay his respects, and when noon came the magistrate had a table of food prepared for him, on which was a dish of skate soup. When the guest saw the soup he twisted his features and refused it, saying, "To-day I am fasting from meat, and so beg to be excused." His face grew very pale, and tears flowed from his eyes. The magistrate thought this behaviour strange, and asked him two or three times the meaning of it. When he could no longer withhold a reply, he went into all the particulars and told him the story.

"Your humble servant," he said, "has in his life met with much unheard-of and unhappy experience, which he has never told to a living soul, but now that your Excellency asks it of me, I cannot refrain from telling. Your servant's father was a very old man, nearly a hundred, when one day he was taken down with a high fever, in which his body was like a fiery furnace. Seeing the danger he was in, his children gathered about weeping, thinking that the time of his departure had surely come. But he lived, and a few days later said to us, 'I am burdened with so great a heat in this sickness that I am not able to endure it longer. I would like to go out to the bank of the river that runs before the house and see the water flowing by, and be refreshed by it. Do not disobey me now, but carry me out at once to the water's edge.'

"We remonstrated with him and begged him not to do so, but he grew very angry, and said, 'If you do not as I command, you will be the death of me'; and so, seeing that there was no help for it, we bore him out and placed him on the bank of the river. He, seeing the water, was greatly delighted, and said, 'The clear flowing water cures my sickness.' A moment later he said further, 'I'd like to be quite alone and rid of you all for a little. Go away into the wood and wait till I tell you to come.'

"We again remonstrated about this, but he grew furiously angry, so that we were helpless. We feared that if we insisted, his sickness would grow worse, and so we were compelled to yield. We went a short distance away and then turned to look, when suddenly the old father was gone from the place where he had been seated. We hurried back to see what had happened. My father had taken off his clothes and plunged into the water, which was muddied. His body was already half metamorphosed into a skate. We saw its transformation in terror, and did not dare to go near him, when all at once it became changed into a great flatfish, that swam and plunged and disported itself in the water with intense delight. He looked back at us as though he could hardly bear to go, but a moment later he was off, entered the deep sea, and did not again appear.

"On the edge of the stream where he had changed his form we found his finger-nails and a tooth. These we buried, and to-day as a family we all abstain from skate fish, and when we see the neighbours frying or eating it we are overcome with disgust and horror."

TOM MOORE
and the SEAL WOMAN

Ireland

In the village of Kilshanig, two miles north-east of Castlegregory, there lived at one time a fine, brave young man named Tom Moore, a good dancer and singer. 'Tis often he was heard singing among the cliffs and in the fields of a night.

Tom's father and mother died and he was alone in the house and in need of a wife. One morning early, when he was at work near the strand, he saw the finest woman ever seen in that part of the kingdom, sitting on a rock, fast asleep. The tide was gone from the rocks then, and Tom was curious to know who was she or what brought her, so he walked toward the rock.

"Wake up!" cried Tom to the woman; "if the tide comes 'twill drown you."

She raised her head and only laughed. Tom left her there, but as he was going he turned every minute to look at the woman. When he came back he caught the spade, but couldn't work; he had to look at the beautiful woman on the rock. At last the tide swept over the rock. He threw the spade down and away to the strand with him, but she slipped into the sea and he saw no more of her that time.

Tom spent the day cursing himself for not taking the woman from the rock when it was God that sent her to him. He couldn't work out the day. He went home.

Tom could not sleep a wink all that night. He was up early next morning and went to the rock. The woman was there. He called to her.

No answer. He went up to the rock. "You may as well come home with me now," said Tom. Not a word from the woman. Tom took the hood from her head and said, "I'll have this!"

The moment be did that she cried: "Give back my hood, Tom Moore!"

"Indeed I will not, for 'twas God sent you to me, and now that you have speech I'm well satisfied! And taking her by the arm he led her to the house. The woman cooked breakfast, and they sat down together to eat it.

"Now," said Tom, "in the name of God you and I'll go to the priest and get married, for the neighbours around here are very watchful; they'd be talking." So after breakfast they went to the priest, and Tom asked him to marry them.

"Where did you get the wife?" asked the priest.

Tom told the whole story. When the priest saw Tom was so anxious to marry be charged £5, and Tom paid the money. He took the wife home with him, and she was as good a woman as ever went into a man's house. She lived with Tom seven years, and had three sons and two daughters.

One day Tom was ploughing, and some part of the plough rigging broke. He thought there were bolts on the loft at home, so he climbed up to get them. He threw down bags and ropes while he was looking for the bolts, and what should he throw down but the hood which he took from the wife seven years before. She saw it the moment it fell, picked it up, and hid it. At that time people heard a great seal roaring out in the sea.

"Ah," said Tom's wife, "that's my brother looking for me."

Some men who were hunting killed three seals that day. All the women of the village ran down to the strand to look at the seals, and Tom's wife with the others. She began to moan, and going up to the dead seals she spoke some words to each and then cried out, "Oh, the murder!"

When they saw her crying the men said: "We'll have nothing more to do with these seals." So they dug a great hole, and the three seals were put into it and covered. But some thought in the night: "Tis a great shame to bury those seals, after all the trouble in taking them." Those men went with shovels and dug up the earth, but found no trace of the seals.

All this time the big seal in the sea was roaring. Next day when Tom was at work his wife swept the house, put everything in order, washed the children and combed their hair; then, taking them one by one, she kissed each. She went next to the rock, and, putting the hood on her head, gave a plunge. That moment the big seal rose and roared so that people ten miles away could hear him.

Tom's wife went away with the seal swimming in the sea. All the five children that she left had webs between their fingers and toes, half-way to the tips.

The descendants of Tom Moore and the seal woman are living near Castle-gregory to this day, and the webs are not gone yet from between their fingers and toes, though decreasing with each generation.

THE FISHERMAN
and HIS WIFE

Germany

There was once on a time a Fisherman who lived with his wife in a miserable hovel close by the sea, and every day he went out fishing. And once as he was sitting with his rod, looking at the clear water, his line suddenly went down, far down below, and when he drew it up again he brought out a large Flounder. Then the Flounder said to him, "Hark, you Fisherman, I pray you, let me live, I am no Flounder really, but an enchanted prince. What good will it do you to kill me? I should not be good to eat, put me in the water again, and let me go." "Come," said the Fisherman, "there is no need for so many words about it—a fish that can talk I should certainly let go, anyhow," with that he put him back again into the clear water, and the Flounder went to the bottom, leaving a long streak of blood behind him. Then the Fisherman got up and went home to his wife in the hovel.

"Husband," said the woman, "have you caught nothing to-day?" "No," said the man, "I did catch a Flounder, who said he was an enchanted prince, so I let him go again." "Did you not wish for anything first?" said the woman. "No," said the man; "what should I wish for?" "Ah," said the woman, "it is surely hard to have to live always in this dirty hovel; you might have wished for a small cottage for us. Go back and call him. Tell him we want to have a small cottage, he will certainly give us that." "Ah," said the man, "why should I go there again?" "Why," said the woman, "you did catch him, and you let him go again; he is sure to do it. Go at once." The man still did not quite like to go, but did not like to oppose his wife, and went to the sea.

When he got there the sea was all green and yellow, and no longer so smooth; so he stood still and said,

"Flounder, flounder in the sea,
Come, I pray thee, here to me;
For my wife, good Ilsabil,
Wills not as I'd have her will."

Then the Flounder came swimming to him and said, "Well what does she want, then?" "Ah," said the man, "I did catch you, and my wife says I really ought to have wished for something. She does not like to live in a wretched hovel any longer. She would like to have a cottage." "Go, then," said the Flounder, "she has it already."

When the man went home, his wife was no longer in the hovel, but instead of it there stood a small cottage, and she was sitting on a bench before the door. Then she took him by the hand and said to him, "Just come inside, look, now isn't this a great deal better?" So they went in, and there was a small porch, and a pretty little parlor and bedroom, and a kitchen and pantry, with the best of furniture, and fitted up with the most beautiful things made of tin and brass, whatsoever was wanted. And behind the cottage there was a small yard, with hens and ducks, and a little garden with flowers and fruit. "Look," said the wife, "is not that nice!" "Yes," said the husband, "and so we must always think it,—now we will live quite contented." "We will think about that," said the wife. With that they ate something and went to bed.

Everything went well for a week or a fortnight, and then the woman said, "Hark you, husband, this cottage is far too small for us, and the garden and yard are little; the Flounder might just as well have given us a larger house. I should like to live in a great stone castle; go to the Flounder, and tell him to give us a castle." "Ah, wife," said the man, "the cottage is quite good enough; why should we live in a castle?" "What!" said the woman; "just go there, the Flounder can always do that." "No, wife," said the man, "the Flounder has just given us the cottage, I do not like to go back so soon, it might make him angry." "Go," said the woman, "he can do it quite easily, and will be glad to do it; just you go to him."

The man's heart grew heavy, and he would not go. He said to himself, "It is not right," and yet he went. And when he came to the sea the water was quite purple and dark-blue, and grey and thick, and no longer so green and yellow, but it was still quiet. And he stood there and said—

"Flounder, flounder in the sea,
Come, I pray thee, here to me;
For my wife, good Ilsabil,
Wills not as I'd have her will."

"Well, what does she want, then?" said the Flounder. "Alas," said the man, half scared, "she wants to live in a great stone castle." "Go to it, then, she is standing before the door," said the Flounder.

Then the man went away, intending to go home, but when he got there, he found a great stone palace, and his wife was just standing on the steps going in, and she took him by the hand and said, "Come in." So he went in with her, and in the castle was a great hall paved with marble, and many servants, who flung wide the doors; And the walls were all bright with beautiful hangings, and in the rooms were chairs and tables of pure gold, and crystal chandeliers hung from the ceiling, and all the rooms and bed-rooms had carpets, and food and wine of the very best were standing on all the tables, so that they nearly broke down beneath it. Behind the house, too, there was a great court-yard, with stables for horses and cows, and the very best of carriages; there was a magnificent large garden, too, with the most beautiful flowers and fruit-trees, and a park quite half a mile long, in which were stags, deer, and hares, and everything that could be desired. "Come," said the woman, "isn't that beautiful?" "Yes, indeed," said the man, "now let it be; and we will live in this beautiful castle and be content." "We will consider about that," said the woman, "and sleep upon it;" thereupon they went to bed.

Next morning the wife awoke first, and it was just daybreak, and from her bed she saw the beautiful country lying before her. Her husband was still stretching himself, so she poked him in the side with her elbow, and said, "Get up, husband, and just peep out of the window. Look you, couldn't we be the King over all that land? Go to the Flounder, we will be the King." "Ah, wife," said the man, "why should we be King? I do not want to be King." "Well," said the wife, "if you won't be King, I will; go to the Flounder, for I will be King." "Ah, wife," said the man, "why do you want to be King? I do not like to say that to him." "Why not?" said the woman; "go to him this instant; I must be King!" So the man went, and was quite unhappy because his wife wished to be King. "It is not right; it is not right," thought he. He did not wish to go, but yet he went.

And when he came to the sea, it was quite dark-grey, and the water heaved up from below, and smelt putrid. Then he went and stood by it, and said,

"Flounder, flounder in the sea,

Come, I pray thee, here to me;

For my wife, good Ilsabil,

Wills not as I'd have her will"

"Well, what does she want, then?" said the Flounder. "Alas," said the man, "she wants to be King." "Go to her; she is King already."

So the man went, and when he came to the palace, the castle had become much larger, and had a great tower and magnificent ornaments, and the sentinel was standing before the door, and there were numbers of soldiers with kettle-drums and trumpets. And when he went inside the house, everything was of real marble and gold, with velvet covers and great golden tassels. Then the doors of the hall were opened, and there was the court in all its splendour, and his wife was sitting on a high throne of gold and diamonds, with a great crown of gold on her head, and a sceptre of pure gold and jewels in her hand, and on both sides of her stood her maids-in-waiting in a row, each of them always one head shorter than the last.

Then he went and stood before her, and said, "Ah, wife, and now you are King." "Yes," said the woman, "now I am King." So he stood and looked at her, and when he had looked at her thus for some time, he said, "And now that you are King, let all else be, now we will wish for nothing more." "Nay, husband," said the woman, quite anxiously, "I find time pass very heavily, I can bear it no longer; go to the Flounder—I am King, but I must be Emperor, too." "Alas, wife, why do you wish to be Emperor?" "Husband," said she, "go to the Flounder. I will be Emperor." "Alas, wife," said the man, "he cannot make you Emperor; I may not say that to the fish. There is only one Emperor in the land. An Emperor the Flounder cannot make you! I assure you he cannot."

"What!" said the woman, "I am the King, and you are nothing but my husband; will you go this moment? go at once! If he can make a King he can make an emperor. I will be Emperor; go instantly." So he was forced to go. As the man went, however, he was troubled in mind, and thought to himself, "It will not end well; it will not end well! Emperor is too shameless! The Flounder will at last be tired out."

With that he reached the sea, and the sea was quite black and thick, and began to boil up from below, so that it threw up bubbles, and such a sharp wind blew over it that it curdled, and the man was afraid. Then he went and stood by it, and said,

"Flounder, flounder in the sea,

Come, I pray thee, here to me;

For my wife, good Ilsabil,

Wills not as I'd have her will."

"Well, what does she want, then?" said the Flounder. "Alas, Flounder," said he, "my wife wants to be Emperor." "Go to her," said the Flounder; "she is Emperor already."

So the man went, and when he got there the whole palace was made of polished marble with alabaster figures and golden ornaments, and soldiers were marching before the door blowing trumpets, and beating cymbals and drums; and in the house, barons, and counts, and dukes were going about as servants. Then they opened the doors to him, which were of pure gold. And when he entered, there sat his wife on a throne, which was made of one piece of gold, and was quite two miles high; and she wore a great golden crown that was three yards high, and set with diamonds and carbuncles, and in one hand she had the sceptre, and in the other the imperial orb; and on both sides of her stood the yeomen of the guard in two rows, each being smaller than the one before him, from the biggest giant, who was two miles high, to the very smallest dwarf, just as big as my little finger. And before it stood a number of princes and dukes.

Then the man went and stood among them, and said, "Wife, are you Emperor now?" "Yes," said she, "now I am Emperor." Then he stood and looked at her well, and when he had looked at her thus for some time, he said, "Ah, wife, be content, now that you are Emperor." "Husband," said she, "why are you standing there? Now, I am Emperor, but I will be Pope too; go to the Flounder." "Alas, wife," said the man, "what will you not wish for? You cannot be Pope. There is but one in Christendom. He cannot make you Pope." "Husband," said she, "I will be Pope; go immediately, I must be Pope this very day." "No, wife," said the man, "I do not like to say that to him; that would not do, it is too much; the Flounder can't make you Pope." "Husband," said she, "what nonsense! If he can make an emperor he can make a pope. Go to him directly. I am Emperor, and you are nothing but my husband; will you go at once?"

Then he was afraid and went; but he was quite faint, and shivered and shook, and his knees and legs trembled. And a high wind blew over the land, and the clouds flew, and towards evening all grew dark, and the leaves fell from the trees, and the water rose and roared as if it were boiling, and splashed upon the shore. And in the distance he saw ships which were firing guns in their sore need, pitching and tossing on the waves. And yet in the midst of the sky there was still a small bit of blue, though on every side it was as red as in a heavy storm. So, full of despair, he went and stood in much fear and said,

"Flounder, flounder in the sea,
Come, I pray thee, here to me;"
For my wife, good Ilsabil,
Wills not as I'd have her will.

"Well, what does she want, then?" said the Flounder. "Alas," said the man, "she wants to be Pope." "Go to her then," said the Flounder; "she is Pope already."

So he went, and when he got there, he saw what seemed to be a large church surrounded by palaces. He pushed his way through the crowd. Inside, however, everything was lighted up with thousands and thousands of candles, and his wife was clad in gold, and she was sitting on a much higher throne, and had three great golden crowns on, and round about her there was much ecclesiastical splendour; and on both sides of her was a row of candles the largest of which was as tall as the very tallest tower, down to the very smallest kitchen candle, and all the emperors and kings were on their knees before her, kissing her shoe. "Wife," said the man, and looked attentively at her, "are you now Pope?" "Yes," said she, "I am Pope." So he stood and looked at her, and it was just as if he was looking at the bright sun. When he had stood looking at her thus for a short time, he said, "Ah, wife, if you are Pope, do let well alone!" But she looked as stiff as a post, and did not move or show any signs of life. Then said he, "Wife, now that you are Pope, be satisfied, you cannot become anything greater now." "I will consider about that," said the woman. Thereupon they both went to bed, but she was not satisfied, and greediness let her have no sleep, for she was continually thinking what there was left for her to be.

The man slept well and soundly, for he had run about a great deal during the day; but the woman could not fall asleep at all, and flung herself from one side to the other the whole night through, thinking always what more was left for her to be, but unable to call to mind anything else. At length the sun began to rise, and when the woman saw the red of dawn, she sat up in bed and looked at it. And when, through the window, she saw the sun thus rising, she said, "Cannot I, too, order the sun and moon to rise?" "Husband," she said, poking him in the ribs with her elbows, "wake up! go to the Flounder, for I wish to be even as God is." The man was still half asleep, but he was so horrified that he fell out of bed. He thought he must have heard amiss, and rubbed his eyes, and said, "Alas, wife, what are you saying?" "Husband," said she, "if I can't order the sun and moon to rise, and have to look on and see the sun and moon rising, I can't bear it. I shall not know what it is to have another happy hour, unless I can make them rise myself." Then she looked at him so terribly that a shudder ran over him, and said, "Go at once; I wish to be like unto God." "Alas, wife," said the man, falling on his knees before her, "the Flounder cannot do that; he can make an emperor and a pope; I beseech you, go on as you are, and be Pope." Then she fell into a rage, and her hair flew wildly about her head, and she cried, "I will not endure this, I'll not bear it any longer; wilt thou go?" Then he put on his trousers and ran away like a madman. But outside a great storm was raging, and blowing so hard that he could scarcely keep his feet; houses and trees toppled over, the mountains trembled, rocks rolled into the sea, the sky was pitch black, and it thundered and lightened, and the sea came in with black waves as high as church-towers and mountains, and all with crests of white foam at the top. Then he cried, but could not hear his own words,

"Flounder, flounder in the sea,
Come, I pray thee, here to me;
For my wife, good Ilsabil,
Wills not as I'd have her will."

"Well, what does she want, then?" said the Flounder. "Alas," said he, "she wants to be like unto God." "Go to her, and you will find her back again in the dirty hovel." And there they are living still at this very time.

TREASURE

THUNDER and ANANSI

Ghana

There had been a long and severe famine in the land where Anansi lived. He had been quite unable to obtain food for his poor wife and family. One day, gazing desperately out to sea, he saw rising from the midst of the water, a tiny island with a tall palm-tree upon it. He determined to reach this tree—if any means proved possible—and climb it, in the hope of finding a few nuts to reward him. How to get there was the difficulty.

This, however, solved itself when he reached the beach, for there lay the means to his hand, in the shape of an old broken boat. It certainly did not look very strong, but Anansi decided to try it.

His first six attempts were unsuccessful—a great wave dashed him back on the beach each time he tried to put off. He was persevering, however, and at the seventh trial was successful in getting away. He steered the battered old boat as best he could, and at length reached the palm-tree of his desire. Having tied the boat to the trunk of the tree—which grew almost straight out of the water—he climbed toward the nuts. Plucking all he could reach, he dropped them, one by one, down to the boat. To his dismay, every one missed the boat and fell, instead, into the water until only the last one remained. This he aimed even more carefully than the others, but it also fell into the water and disappeared from his hungry eyes. He had not tasted even one and now all were gone.

He could not bear the thought of going home empty-handed, so, in his despair, he threw himself into the water, too. To his complete astonishment, instead of being drowned, he found himself standing on the sea-bottom in front of a pretty little cottage. From the latter came an old man, who asked Anansi what he wanted so badly that he had come to Thunder's cottage to seek it. Anansi told his tale of woe, and Thunder showed himself most sympathetic.

He went into the cottage and fetched a fine cooking-pot, which he presented to Anansi—telling him that he need never be hungry again. The pot would always supply enough food for himself and his family. Anansi was most grateful, and left Thunder with many thanks.

Being anxious to test the pot at once, Anansi only waited till he was again seated in the old boat to say, "Pot, pot, what you used to do for your master do now for me." Immediately good food of all sorts appeared. Anansi ate a hearty meal, which he very much enjoyed.

On reaching land again, his first thought was to run home and give all his family a good meal from his wonderful pot. A selfish, greedy fear prevented him. "What if I should use up all the magic of the pot on them, and have nothing more left for myself! Better keep the pot a secret—then I can enjoy a meal when I want one." So, his mind full of this thought, he hid the pot.

He reached home, pretending to be utterly worn out with fatigue and hunger. There was not a grain of food to be had anywhere. His wife and poor children were weak with want of it, but selfish Anansi took no notice of that. He congratulated himself at the thought of his magic pot, now safely hidden in his room. There he retired from time to time when he felt hungry, and enjoyed a good meal. His family got thinner and thinner, but he grew plumper and plumper. They began to suspect some secret, and determined to find it out. His eldest son, Kweku Tsin, had the power of changing himself into any shape he chose; so he took the form of a tiny fly, and accompanied his father everywhere. At last, Anansi, feeling hungry, entered his room and closed the door. Next he took the pot, and had a fine meal. Having replaced the pot in its hiding-place, he went out, on the pretence of looking for food.

As soon as he was safely out of sight, Kweku Tsin fetched out the pot and called all his hungry family to come at once. They had as good a meal as their father had had. When they had finished, Mrs. Anansi—to punish her husband—said she would take the pot down to the village and give everybody a meal. This she did—but alas! in working to prepare so much food at one time, the pot grew too hot and melted away. What was to be done now? Anansi would be so angry! His wife forbade every one to mention the pot.

Anansi returned, ready for his supper, and, as usual, went into his room, carefully shutting the door. He went to the hiding-place—it was empty. He looked around in consternation. No pot was to be seen anywhere. Some one must have discovered it. His family must be the culprits; he would find a means to punish them.

Saying nothing to any one about the matter, he waited till morning. As soon as it was light he started off towards the shore, where the old boat lay. Getting into the boat, it started of its own accord and glided swiftly over the water—straight for the palm-tree. Arrived there, Anansi attached the boat as before and climbed the tree. This time, unlike the last, the nuts almost fell into his hands. When he aimed them at the boat they fell easily into it—not one, as before, dropping into the water. He deliberately took them and threw them overboard, immediately jumping after them. As before, he found himself in front of Thunder's cottage, with Thunder waiting to hear his tale. This he told, the old man showing the same sympathy as he had previously done.

This time, however, he presented Anansi with a fine stick and bade him good-bye. Anansi could scarcely wait till he got into the boat—so anxious was he to try the magic properties of his new gift. "Stick, stick," he said, "what you used to do for your master do for me also." The stick began to beat him so severely that, in a few minutes, he was obliged to jump into the water and swim ashore, leaving boat and stick to drift away where they pleased. Then he returned sorrowfully homeward, bemoaning his many bruises and wishing he had acted more wisely from the beginning.

BENITO, the FAITHFUL SERVANT

The Philippines

On a time there lived in a village a poor man and his wife, who had a son named Benito. The one ambition of the lad from his earliest youth was that he might be a help to the family in their struggle for a living.

But the years went by, and he saw no opportunity until one day, as they sat at dinner, his father fell to talking about the young King who lived at a distance from the village, in a beautiful palace kept by a retinue of servants. The boy was glad to hear this, and asked his parents to let him become one of the servants of this great ruler. The mother protested, fearing that her son could not please his Royal Majesty; but the boy was so eager to try his fortune that at last he was permitted to do so.

The next day his mother prepared food for him to eat on the journey, and he started for the palace. The journey was tiresome; and when he reached the palace he had difficulty in obtaining an audience with the King. But when he succeeded and made known his wish, the monarch detected a charming personality hidden within the ragged clothes, and, believing the lad would make a willing servant, he accepted him.

The servants of his Majesty had many duties. Theirs was not a life of ease, but of hard work. The very next day the King called Benito, and said, "I want you to bring me a certain beautiful princess who lives in a land across the sea; and if you fail to do it, you will be punished."

Benito did not know how he was to do it; but he asked no questions, and unhesitatingly answered, "I will, my lord."

That same day he provided himself with everything he needed for the journey and set off. He travelled a long distance until he came to the heart of a thick forest, where he saw a large bird which said to him, "Oh, my friend! please take away these strings that are wrapped all about me. If you will, I will help you whenever you call upon me."

Benito released the bird and asked it its name. It replied, "Sparrow-hawk," and flew away. Benito continued his journey until he came to the seashore. There he could see no way of getting across, and, remembering what the King had said if he failed, he stood looking out over the sea, feeling very sad. The huge King of the Fishes saw him, and swam toward him. "Why are you so sad?" asked the Fish.

"I wish to cross the sea to find the beautiful Princess," replied the youth.

"Get on my back and I will take you across," said the King of the Fishes.

Benito rode on the back of the Fish and crossed the sea. As soon as he reached the other side, a fairy in the form of a woman appeared to him, and became a great aid to him in his adventure. She knew exactly what he wanted; so she told him that the Princess was shut up in a castle guarded by giants, and that he would have to fight the giants before he could reach her. For this purpose she gave him a magic sword, which would kill on the instant anything it touched.

Benito now felt sure he could take the Princess from her cruel guardsmen. He went to the castle, and there he saw many giants round about it. When the giants saw him coming, they went out to meet him, thinking to take him captive. They were so sure that they could easily do it, that they went forth unarmed. As they came near, he touched the foremost ones with his sword, and one after another they fell down dead. The other giants, seeing so many of their number slain, became terrified, and fled, leaving the castle unguarded.

The young man went to the Princess and told her that his master had sent him to bring her to his palace. The young Princess was only too glad to leave the land of the giants, where she had been held captive. So the two set out together for the King's palace.

When they came to the sea they rode across it on the back of the same fish that had carried Benito. They went through the forest, and at last came to the palace. Here they were received with the greatest rejoicings.

After a short time the King asked the Princess to become his wife. "I will, O King!" she replied, "if you will get the ring I lost in the sea as I was crossing it."

The monarch called Benito, and ordered him to find the ring which had been lost on their journey from the land of the giants.

Obedient to his master, Benito started, and travelled on and on till he came to the shore of the sea. There he stood, gazing sadly out over the waters, not knowing how he was to search for what lay at the bottom of the deep ocean.

Again the King of the Fishes came to him, asking the cause of his sadness. Benito replied, "The Princess lost her ring while we were crossing the sea, and I have been sent to find it."

The King-Fish summoned all the fishes to come to him. When they had assembled, he noticed that one was missing. He commanded the others to search for this one, and bring it to him. They found it under a stone, and it said, "I am so full! I have eaten so much that I cannot swim." So the larger ones took it by the tail and dragged it to their King.

"Why did you not come when summoned?" asked the King-Fish. "I was so full I could not swim," replied the Fish.

The King-Fish, suspecting that it had swallowed the ring, ordered it to be cut in two. The others cut it open, and, behold! there was the lost ornament. Benito thanked the King of the Fishes, took the ring, and brought it to the monarch.

When the great ruler got the ring, he said to the Princess, "Now that I have your ring, will you become my wife?"

"I will be your wife," replied the Princess, "if you will find the earring I lost in the forest as I was journeying with Benito."

Instantly Benito was called, and was ordered to find the lost jewel. He was very weary from his former journey; but, mindful of his duty, he started for the forest, reaching it before the day was over. He searched for the earring faithfully, following the road which he and the Princess had taken; but all in vain. He was much discouraged, and sat down under a tree to rest. To his surprise a mouse of monstrous size appeared before him. It was the King of the Mice.

"Why are you so sad?" asked the Mouse.

"I am searching for an earring which the Princess lost as we passed through the forest, but am unable to find it."

"I will find it for you," said the King-Mouse.

Benito's face brightened at hearing this. The King-Mouse called all his followers, and all but one little mouse responded. Then the King of the Mice ordered some of his subjects to find the absent one. They found him in a small hole among the bamboo-trees. He said he could not go because he was so satisfied (sated). So the others pulled him along to their master; and he, finding that there was something hard within the little mouse, ordered him to be cut open. It was done; and there was the very earring for which the tired servant was looking. Benito took it, thanked the King of the Mice, and brought the earring to his own King.

When the monarch received it, he immediately restored it to its owner and asked, "Will you now become my wife?"

"Oh, dear King!" responded the Princess, "I have only one more thing to ask of you; and if you will grant it, I will be your wife forever."

The King, pleased with his former successes, said, "Tell me what it is, and it shall be granted."

"If you will get some water from heaven," said the Princess, "and some water from the nether-world, I will become your wife. That is my last wish."

The King called Benito, and commanded him to get water from these two places. "I will, my King," said Benito; and he took some provisions and started. He came to the forest; but there he became confused, for he did not know in which direction to go to reach either of the places. Suddenly he recalled the promise of the bird he had helped the first time he entered the wood. He called the bird, and it soon appeared. He told it what he wanted, and it said, "I will get it for you."

He made two cups of bamboo, and tied one to each of the bird's legs. They were very light, and did not hinder the bearer at all. Away the bird flew, going very fast. Before the day was ended, it came back with each cup full of water, and told

Benito that the one tied to its right leg contained water from heaven, and the one tied to its left leg contained water from the nether-world.

Benito untied the cups, taking great care of them. He was about to leave, when the bird asked him to tarry long enough to bury it, as the places to which it had been were so far away that it was weary unto death.

Benito did not like to bury the bird, but he soon saw that it really was dying, so he waited; and when it was dead, he buried it, feeling very sorry over the loss of so helpful a friend.

He went back to the palace and delivered the two kinds of water to his master. The Princess then asked the King to cut her in two and pour the water from heaven upon her. The King was not willing to do it, so she did it herself, asking the King to pour the water. This he did, and, lo! the Princess turned into the most beautiful woman that ever the sun shone on.

Then the King was desirous of becoming handsome; so he asked the Princess to pour the other cup of water over him after he cut himself. He cut himself, and she poured over his body the water from the nether-world; but from him there arose a spirit more ugly and ill-favored than imagination could picture. Fortunately, it soon vanished from sight.

The Princess then turned to Benito, and said, "You have been faithful in your duties to your master, kind to me in restoring the jewels I lost, and brave in delivering me from the cruel giants. You are the man I choose for my husband."

Benito could not refuse so lovely a lady. They were married amid great festivities, and became the king and queen of that broad and fertile land.

Benito gave his parents one of the finest portions of his kingdom, and furnished them with everything they could desire. From that time on they were all very happy,—so happy that the story of their bliss has come down through the centuries to us.

THE BLACK PEARL

Bahrain

One day when Amry, the pearl-diver, had gone to the shop of the court jeweller of Oman, to sell him the pearls he had found beneath the waters of the isle of Bahrein[1], the beautiful Anouba, wife of the sultan, stopped her palanquin at the merchant's door. Coming toward him, she held out a wonderful black pearl, from which the light drew golden reflections.

"Have you a pearl to match this which you can sell me?" she asked.

The jeweller took the pearl, laid it on a cushion of silk and studied it, his hands crossed upon his breast, like a Brahmin adoring his god. And then he shook his head with discouragement and replied, "This pearl has no equal in the world." And Amry, who had drawn near, softly echoed the merchant's words.

"Then it would be useless for me to try to find the mate of this pearl of mine?" asked the beautiful Anouba.

"Princess," replied the merchant, bowing to the ground, "ask me for emeralds as large as pigeons' eggs, ask me for translucent jade-stones, ask me for cabochons of topaz, glowing like tigers' eyes, and for those rubies of Ceylon which shed fire by night. Those, by the mercy of Allah, your slave can lay at your feet! Yet before another pearl like yours be found, the stars of heaven will fall in a shower of gold on your palace roof!" While they spoke the Princess who had glanced round the

---

1. An archaic spelling.

shop from beneath her veil, noticed that Amry, leaning against a bamboo pillar, was looking at the pearl.

"Is this man your slave?" the beautiful Anouba asked the merchant.

Amry proudly raised his head. "I am Amry, the pearl-diver. The son of the sea is no man's slave!"

"Amry," said Anouba, "do you also say that the equal of my black pearl cannot be found?"

"In a bay of the island of Bahrein," said Amry, "two hundred feet under water, lies a coral-reef on which old Phangar, the most famous diver of the Gulf, found the black pearl which Prince Meschad wears in the pommel of his dagger. It is possible that the mate to your pearl might be found there. But Phangar never again dived into that abyss, and he trembles with terror when he passes over it in his boat."

"Why should he tremble?" asked Anouba, filled with curiosity.

"When Phangar, his left foot clinging to the leaden weight which carried him to the bottom, shot through the water, he passed through a whirlpool of green waves which boiled and swirled around him like the lava of the volcanoes. So great was the shock that when his plummet reached bottom he fell forward on his hands and knees. Yet, though the sharp points of the coral, whose cut pricks like hot iron, drew blood from a hundred wounds, he did not complain. He at once set to work, and had already gathered a hundred oysters in his linen bag when it seemed as though the whole reef were rising around him, and a floating mass, gray like the coral itself, advanced slowly toward him, stretching forth long tentacles as flexible as forest creepers. One of these tentacles touched Phangar's breast and attached itself there, but Phangar could not cry out. A gigantic squid, floating but a few yards away from him, had fixed him with its pale green eyes, luminous with a cold flame.

"When Phangar's comrades, who had remained in the boat, felt his life-line suddenly stiffen, they hastened to draw him to the surface—only just in time. The diver had lost consciousness, and on his breast was the mark left by the squid. Three days later, when he opened the pearls he had brought up, one of them contained the superb black pearl which Prince Meschid afterwards bought for a fabulous price."

"That is well," said the sultan's wife. "Since you know where the black pearls are to be found, you must plunge in the Gulf of Bahrein for me, descend to the coral-reef, slay the monster who guards the treasure, and bring back the pearl I desire."

Amry replied, "Who knows whether there are two pearls equally matched in all the seas of the world? And why should I risk my life to satisfy your caprice, even though you be the sultan's wife? Yet for the sake of my mother, who is old and infirm, and whom I would fain take far from this sea-coast, whose air lies heavy on her lungs, I will dive for you for a price."

"What is the price you ask?" queried the Princess Anouba.

"No less than twenty thousand pieces of gold," said Amry.

"So be it," replied Anouba. "You ask a great sum. Yet, if you can bring me a pearl as large and beautiful as this, then you shall have the twenty thousand pieces of gold."

And Amry said, "I will go to seek the black pearl at the bottom of the abyss of Bahrein, even though I have to leave my flesh and bones on the craggy points of the coral-reef."

The following day, after having taken leave of his aged mother, to whom he said nothing of his intentions, however, Amry took his boat and set off in the direction in which he knew the treasure was to be found. When he had shot to the bottom of the sea, he made haste to fill his linen bag with the largest and finest oysters on the reef. And then, just as he was about to rise once more to the surface, he saw in a rocky niche, an oyster of monster size. He stretched forth his hand and grasped it, and at that moment the giant squid which made its home on the coral bank, suddenly wound its tentacles around him. Amry seemed lost. Yet Allah the Compassionate watches over those who honor their parents! He does not suffer them to go down to destruction. From the heights of his golden, irradiant throne in Paradise, whose light is like a glistening star, the omniscient eye of Allah beheld Amry struggling beneath the gloomy waters of the sea with the squid. Slightly, very slightly, Allah nodded his head, and angels in their thousands, to whom Allah's unspoken thought comes with the clear sweetness of a celestial voice, hastened to do his bidding. At either hand they thrust back the clouds which hid it from the sight of man, and for one brief moment the light of Allah's throne was unveiled in all its ineffable brightness. And in that moment, before the clouds closed round the throne again, its light clove through the spaces of the seven heavens, through the airs of earth and the water of the sea. Like a sword of flame it struck the monster beneath the waves, who, as it touched it, turned into a black and shrivelled mass.

Amry, released from the embrace which was suffocating him, knew who had intervened on his behalf, and his last waking thought was a prayer of gratitude to Allah the Merciful. His linen bag had been torn from him in the struggle with the squid, but when his comrades drew him to the surface of the water, torn, bleeding and unconscious, he still held tightly clasped in his hand the monstrous oyster he had torn from the rock a few moments before.

When he opened the oyster in his humble home, behold, it contained a pearl even larger and more beautiful than that of the Princess Anouba, with reflections even more golden than those of the gem set in the hilt of Prince Meschid's dagger!

In the morning he took it to the sultan's palace, and when the Princess Anouba had seen and examined it, she clapped her hands with delight, called for the treasurer, and Amry's twenty thousand pieces of gold were counted out to him forthwith. Never did Amry plunge for pearls again. A rich man, he took his aged mother to the pleasant city of Yemen, where he bought a fine house in whose rose-gardens the nightingales sang, and the voice of the sea was never heard. There his mother recovered her health, and he himself married and lived happily for many a long year.

THE STORY of URASHIMA TARO, the FISHER LAD

Japan

Long, long ago in the province of Tango there lived on the shore of Japan in the little fishing village of Mizu-no-ye a young fisherman named Urashima Taro. His father had been a fisherman before him, and his skill had more than doubly descended to his son, for Urashima was the most skillful fisher in all that country side, and could catch more Bonito and Tai in a day than his comrades could in a week.

But in the little fishing village, more than for being a clever fisher of the sea was he known for his kind heart. In his whole life he had never hurt anything, either great or small, and when a boy, his companions had always laughed at him, for he would never join with them in teasing animals, but always tried to keep them from this cruel sport.

One soft summer twilight he was going home at the end of a day's fishing when he came upon a group of children. They were all screaming and talking at the tops of their voices, and seemed to be in a state of great excitement about something, and on his going up to them to see what was the matter he saw that they were tormenting a tortoise. First one boy pulled it this way, then another boy pulled it that way, while a third child beat it with a stick, and the fourth hammered its shell with a stone.

Now Urashima felt very sorry for the poor tortoise and made up his mind to rescue it. He spoke to the boys:

"Look here, boys, you are treating that poor tortoise so badly that it will soon die!"

The boys, who were all of an age when children seem to delight in being cruel to animals, took no notice of Urashima's gentle reproof, but went on teasing it as before. One of the older boys answered:

"Who cares whether it lives or dies? We do not. Here, boys, go on, go on!"

And they began to treat the poor tortoise more cruelly than ever. Urashima waited a moment, turning over in his mind what would be the best way to deal with the boys. He would try to persuade them to give the tortoise up to him, so he smiled at them and said:

"I am sure you are all good, kind boys! Now won't you give me the tortoise? I should like to have it so much!"

"No, we won't give you the tortoise," said one of the boys. "Why should we? We caught it ourselves."

"What you say is true," said Urashima, "but I do not ask you to give it to me for nothing. I will give you some money for it—in other words, the Ojisan (Uncle) will buy it of you. Won't that do for you, my boys?" He held up the money to them, strung on a piece of string through a hole in the center of each coin. "Look, boys, you can buy anything you like with this money. You can do much more with this money than you can with that poor tortoise. See what good boys you are to listen to me."

The boys were not bad boys at all, they were only mischievous, and as Urashima spoke they were won by his kind smile and gentle words and began "to be of his spirit," as they say in Japan. Gradually they all came up to him, the ringleader of the little band holding out the tortoise to him.

"Very well, Ojisan, we will give you the tortoise if you will give us the money!" And Urashima took the tortoise and gave the money to the boys, who, calling to each other, scampered away and were soon out of sight.

Then Urashima stroked the tortoise's back, saying as he did so:

"Oh, you poor thing! Poor thing!—there, there! you are safe now! They say that a stork lives for a thousand years, but the tortoise for ten thousand years. You have the longest life of any creature in this world, and you were in great danger of having that precious life cut short by those cruel boys. Luckily I was passing by and saved you, and so life is still yours. Now I am going to take you back to your home, the sea, at once. Do not let yourself be caught again, for there might be no one to save you next time!"

All the time that the kind fisherman was speaking he was walking quickly to the shore and out upon the rocks; then putting the tortoise into the water he watched the animal disappear, and turned homewards himself, for he was tired and the sun had set.

The next morning Urashima went out as usual in his boat. The weather was fine and the sea and sky were both blue and soft in the tender haze of the summer morning. Urashima got into his boat and dreamily pushed out to sea, throwing his line as he did so. He soon passed the other fishing boats and left them behind him till they were lost to sight in the distance, and his boat drifted further and further out upon the blue waters. Somehow, he knew not why, he felt unusually happy that morning; and he could not help wishing that, like the tortoise he set free the day before, he had thousands of years to live instead of his own short span of human life.

He was suddenly startled from his reverie by hearing his own name called:

"Urashima, Urashima!"

Clear as a bell and soft as the summer wind the name floated over the sea.

He stood up and looked in every direction, thinking that one of the other boats had overtaken him, but gaze as he might over the wide expanse of water, near or far there was no sign of a boat, so the voice could not have come from any human being.

Startled, and wondering who or what it was that had called him so clearly, he looked in all directions round about him and saw that without his knowing it a tortoise had come to the side of the boat. Urashima saw with surprise that it was the very tortoise he had rescued the day before.

"Well, Mr. Tortoise," said Urashima, "was it you who called my name just now?"

The tortoise nodded its head several times and said:

"Yes, it was I. Yesterday in your honorable shadow (o kage sama de) my life was saved, and I have come to offer you my thanks and to tell you how grateful I am for your kindness to me."

"Indeed," said Urashima, "that is very polite of you. Come up into the boat. I would offer you a smoke, but as you are a tortoise doubtless you do not smoke," and the fisherman laughed at the joke.

"He-he-he-he!" laughed the tortoise; "sake (rice wine) is my favorite refreshment, but I do not care for tobacco."

"Indeed," said Urashima, "I regret very much that I have no "sake" in my boat to offer you, but come up and dry your back in the sun—tortoises always love to do that."

So the tortoise climbed into the boat, the fisherman helping him, and after an exchange of complimentary speeches the tortoise said:

"Have you ever seen Rin Gin, the Palace of the Dragon King of the Sea, Urashima?"

The fisherman shook his head and replied; "No; year after year the sea has been my home, but though I have often heard of the Dragon King's realm under the sea I have never yet set eyes on that wonderful place. It must be very far away, if it exists at all!"

"Is that really so? You have never seen the Sea King's Palace? Then you have missed seeing one of the most wonderful sights in the whole universe. It is far away at the bottom of the sea, but if I take you there we shall soon reach the place. If you would like to see the Sea King's land I will be your guide."

"I should like to go there, certainly, and you are very kind to think of taking me, but you must remember that I am only a poor mortal and have not the power of swimming like a sea creature such as you are—"

Before the fisherman could say more the tortoise stopped him, saying:

"What? You need not swim yourself. If you will ride on my back I will take you without any trouble on your part."

"But," said Urashima, "how is it possible for me to ride on your small back?"

"It may seem absurd to you, but I assure you that you can do so. Try at once! Just come and get on my back, and see if it is as impossible as you think!"

As the tortoise finished speaking, Urashima looked at its shell, and strange to say he saw that the creature had suddenly grown so big that a man could easily sit on its back.

"This is strange indeed!" said Urashima; "then, Mr. Tortoise, with your kind permission I will get on your back. Dokoisho!"[1] he exclaimed as he jumped on.

The tortoise, with an unmoved face, as if this strange proceeding were quite an ordinary event, said:

"Now we will set out at our leisure," and with these words he leapt into the sea with Urashima on his back. Down through the water the tortoise dived. For a long time these two strange companions rode through the sea. Urashima never grew tired, nor his clothes moist with the water. At last, far away in the distance a magnificent gate appeared, and behind the gate, the long, sloping roofs of a palace on the horizon.

"Ya," exclaimed Urashima. "That looks like the gate of some large palace just appearing! Mr. Tortoise, can you tell what that place is we can now see?"

"That is the great gate of the Rin Gin Palace, the large roof that you see behind the gate is the Sea King's Palace itself."

"Then we have at last come to the realm of the Sea King and to his Palace," said Urashima.

"Yes, indeed," answered the tortoise, "and don't you think we have come very quickly?" And while he was speaking the tortoise reached the side of the gate. "And here we are, and you must please walk from here."

The tortoise now went in front, and speaking to the gatekeeper, said:

"This is Urashima Taro, from the country of Japan. I have had the honor of bringing him as a visitor to this kingdom. Please show him the way."

Then the gatekeeper, who was a fish, at once led the way through the gate before them.

The red bream, the flounder, the sole, the cuttlefish, and all the chief vassals of the Dragon King of the Sea now came out with courtly bows to welcome the stranger.

---

1. "All right" (only used by lower classes).

"Urashima Sama, Urashima Sama! welcome to the Sea Palace, the home of the Dragon King of the Sea. Thrice welcome are you, having come from such a distant country. And you, Mr. Tortoise, we are greatly indebted to you for all your trouble in bringing Urashima here." Then, turning again to Urashima, they said, "Please follow us this way," and from here the whole band of fishes became his guides.

Urashima, being only a poor fisher lad, did not know how to behave in a palace; but, strange though it was all to him, he did not feel ashamed or embarrassed, but followed his kind guides quite calmly where they led to the inner palace. When he reached the portals a beautiful Princess with her attendant maidens came out to welcome him. She was more beautiful than any human being, and was robed in flowing garments of red and soft green like the under side of a wave, and golden threads glimmered through the folds of her gown. Her lovely black hair streamed over her shoulders in the fashion of a king's daughter many hundreds of years ago, and when she spoke her voice sounded like music over the water. Urashima was lost in wonder while he looked upon her, and he could not speak. Then he remembered that he ought to bow, but before he could make a low obeisance the Princess took him by the hand and led him to a beautiful hall, and to the seat of honor at the upper end, and bade him be seated.

"Urashima Taro, it gives me the highest pleasure to welcome you to my father's kingdom," said the Princess. "Yesterday you set free a tortoise, and I have sent for you to thank you for saving my life, for I was that tortoise. Now if you like you shall live here forever in the land of eternal youth, where summer never dies and where sorrow never comes, and I will be your bride if you will, and we will live together happily forever afterwards!"

And as Urashima listened to her sweet words and gazed upon her lovely face his heart was filled with a great wonder and joy, and he answered her, wondering if it was not all a dream:

"Thank you a thousand times for your kind speech. There is nothing I could wish for more than to be permitted to stay here with you in this beautiful land, of which I have often heard, but have never seen to this day. Beyond all words, this is the most wonderful place I have ever seen."

While he was speaking a train of fishes appeared, all dressed in ceremonial, trailing garments. One by one, silently and with stately steps, they entered the hall, bearing on coral trays delicacies of fish and seaweed, such as no one can dream of, and this wondrous feast was set before the bride and bridegroom. The bridal was celebrated with dazzling splendor, and in the Sea King's realm there was great rejoicing. As soon as the young pair had pledged themselves in the wedding cup of wine, three times three, music was played, and songs were sung, and fishes with silver scales and golden tails stepped in from the waves and danced. Urashima enjoyed himself with all his heart. Never in his whole life had he sat down to such a marvelous feast.

When the feast was over the Princes asked the bridegroom if he would like to walk through the palace and see all there was to be seen. Then the happy fisherman, following his bride, the Sea King's daughter, was shown all the wonders of that enchanted land where youth and joy go hand in hand and neither time nor age can touch them. The palace was built of coral and adorned with pearls, and the beauties and wonders of the place were so great that the tongue fails to describe them.

But, to Urashima, more wonderful than the palace was the garden that surrounded it. Here was to be seen at one time the scenery of the four different seasons; the beauties of summer and winter, spring and autumn, were displayed to the wondering visitor at once.

First, when he looked to the east, the plum and cherry trees were seen in full bloom, the nightingales sang in the pink avenues, and butterflies flitted from flower to flower.

Looking to the south all the trees were green in the fullness of summer, and the day cicala and the night cricket chirruped loudly.

Looking to the west the autumn maples were ablaze like a sunset sky, and the chrysanthemums were in perfection.

Looking to the north the change made Urashima start, for the ground was silver white with snow, and trees and bamboos were also covered with snow and the pond was thick with ice.

And each day there were new joys and new wonders for Urashima, and so great was his happiness that he forgot everything, even the home he had left behind and his parents and his own country, and three days passed without his even thinking of all he had left behind. Then his mind came back to him and he remembered who he was, and that he did not belong to this wonderful land or the Sea King's palace, and he said to himself:

"O dear! I must not stay on here, for I have an old father and mother at home. What can have happened to them all this time? How anxious they must have been these days when I did not return as usual. I must go back at once without letting one more day pass." And he began to prepare for the journey in great haste.

Then he went to his beautiful wife, the Princess, and bowing low before her he said:

"Indeed, I have been very happy with you for a long time, Otohime Sama" (for that was her name), "and you have been kinder to me than any words can tell. But now I must say good-by. I must go back to my old parents."

Then Otohime Sama began to weep, and said softly and sadly:

"Is it not well with you here, Urashima, that you wish to leave me so soon? Where is the haste? Stay with me yet another day only!"

But Urashima had remembered his old parents, and in Japan the duty to parents is stronger than everything else, stronger even than pleasure or love, and he would not be persuaded, but answered:

"Indeed, I must go. Do not think that I wish to leave you. It is not that. I must go and see my old parents. Let me go for one day and I will come back to you."

"Then," said the Princess sorrowfully, "there is nothing to be done. I will send you back to-day to your father and mother, and instead of trying to keep you with me one more day, I shall give you this as a token of our love—please take it back with you;" and she brought him a beautiful lacquer box tied about with a silken cord and tassels of red silk.

Urashima had received so much from the Princess already that he felt some compunction in taking the gift, and said:

"It does not seem right for me to take yet another gift from you after all the many favors I have received at your hands, but because it is your wish I will do so," and then he added:

"Tell me what is this box?"

"That," answered the Princess "is the tamate-bako (Box of the Jewel Hand), and it contains something very precious. You must not open this box, whatever happens! If you open it something dreadful will happen to you! Now promise me that you will never open this box!"

And Urashima promised that he would never, never open the box whatever happened.

Then bidding good-by to Otohime Sama he went down to the seashore, the Princess and her attendants following him, and there he found a large tortoise waiting for him.

He quickly mounted the creature's back and was carried away over the shining sea into the East. He looked back to wave his hand to Otohime Sama till at last he could see her no more, and the land of the Sea King and the roofs of the wonderful palace were lost in the far, far distance. Then, with his face turned eagerly towards his own land, he looked for the rising of the blue hills on the horizon before him.

At last the tortoise carried him into the bay he knew so well, and to the shore from whence he had set out. He stepped on to the shore and looked about him while the tortoise rode away back to the Sea King's realm.

But what is the strange fear that seizes Urashima as he stands and looks about him? Why does he gaze so fixedly at the people that pass him by, and why do they in turn stand and look at him? The shore is the same and the hills are the same, but the people that he sees walking past him have very different faces to those he had known so well before.

Wondering what it can mean he walks quickly towards his old home. Even that looks different, but a house stands on the spot, and he calls out:

"Father, I have just returned!" and he was about to enter, when he saw a strange man coming out.

"Perhaps my parents have moved while I have been away, and have gone some-where else," was the fisherman's thought. Somehow he began to feel strangely anxious, he could not tell why.

"Excuse me," said he to the man who was staring at him, "but till within the last few days I have lived in this house. My name is Urashima Taro. Where have my parents gone whom I left here?"

A very bewildered expression came over the face of the man, and, still gazing intently on Urashima's face, he said:

"What? Are you Urashima Taro?"

"Yes," said the fisherman, "I am Urashima Taro!"

"Ha, ha!" laughed the man, "you must not make such jokes. It is true that once upon a time a man called Urashima Taro did live in this village, but that is a story three hundred years old. He could not possibly be alive now!"

When Urashima heard these strange words he was frightened, and said:

"Please, please, you must not joke with me, I am greatly perplexed. I am really Urashima Taro, and I certainly have not lived three hundred years. Till four or five days ago I lived on this spot. Tell me what I want to know without more joking, please."

But the man's face grew more and more grave, and he answered:

"You may or may not be Urashima Taro, I don't know. But the Urashima Taro of whom I have heard is a man who lived three hundred years ago. Perhaps you are his spirit come to revisit your old home?"

"Why do you mock me?" said Urashima. "I am no spirit! I am a living man—do you not see my feet;" and "don-don," he stamped on the ground, first with one foot and then with the other to show the man. (Japanese ghosts have no feet.)

"But Urashima Taro lived three hundred years ago, that is all I know; it is written in the village chronicles," persisted the man, who could not believe what the fisherman said.

Urashima was lost in bewilderment and trouble. He stood looking all around him, terribly puzzled, and, indeed, something in the appearance of everything was different to what he remembered before he went away, and the awful feeling came over him that what the man said was perhaps true. He seemed to be in a strange dream. The few days he had spent in the Sea King's palace beyond the sea had not been days at all: they had been hundreds of years, and in that time his parents had died and all the people he had ever known, and the village had written down his story. There was no use in staying here any longer. He must get back to his beautiful wife beyond the sea.

He made his way back to the beach, carrying in his hand the box which the Princess had given him. But which was the way? He could not find it alone! Suddenly he remembered the box, the tamate-bako.

"The Princess told me when she gave me the box never to open it—that it contained a very precious thing. But now that I have no home, now that I have lost everything that was dear to me here, and my heart grows thin with sadness, at such a time, if I open the box, surely I shall find something that will help me, something that will show me the way back to my beautiful Princess over the sea. There is nothing else for me to do now. Yes, yes, I will open the box and look in!"

And so his heart consented to this act of disobedience, and he tried to persuade himself that he was doing the right thing in breaking his promise.

Slowly, very slowly, he untied the red silk cord, slowly and wonderingly he lifted the lid of the precious box. And what did he find? Strange to say only a beautiful little purple cloud rose out of the box in three soft wisps. For an instant it covered his face and wavered over him as if loath to go, and then it floated away like vapor over the sea.

Urashima, who had been till that moment like a strong and handsome youth of twenty-four, suddenly became very, very old. His back doubled up with age, his hair turned snowy white, his face wrinkled and he fell down dead on the beach.

Poor Urashima! because of his disobedience he could never return to the Sea King's realm or the lovely Princess beyond the sea.

Little children, never be disobedient to those who are wiser than you for disobedience was the beginning of all the miseries and sorrows of life.

A NOTE ON THE SOURCES

The stories in this book were collected, translated, and published in the late nineteenth and early twentieth centuries. They have been excerpted from the following publications, all of which are in the public domain.

In most cases, the authors either completed the transcription and translation themselves or worked with unnamed interpreters. The storytellers also generally go unnamed. In most cases, all the available information on authorship is given in the source list on the following page. But in a few cases, we have more information:

Thomas G. Thrum credits "Kahalaopuna, Princess of Manoa" to Emma Kailikapuolono Metcalf Beckley Nakuina.

Yei Theodora Ozaki notes that "The Story of Urashima Taro, the Fisher Lad" is translated from an original version by Sadanami Sanjin.

James S. Gale's translation of "The Old Man Who Became a Fish" is based on the original of Im Bang.

And Frederick Herman Martens adapted "The Black Pearl" from *Les Merveilles de l'Inde (Adja ib AL-Hind)* by Alphonse Lemerre, which is itself a translation of a tenth century Arabic manuscript.

SOURCES

Benito, the Faithful Servant
Kern Bayliss, Clara. "Philippine Folk-Tales." *The Journal of American Folklore,* 1908. Internet Archive, 2013. https://archive.org/details/jstor-534529/page/n4/mode/2up.

The Betrothed of Destiny
Seklemian, A. G. *The Golden Maiden and Other Folk Tales and Fairy Stories Told in Armenia.* Cleveland and New York: The Helman-Taylor Company, 1898. Internet Archive, 2018. https://archive.org/details/Seklemian1898ArmenianTales/page/n9/mode/2up.

The Black Pearl
Martens, Frederick H. *Fairy Tales from the Orient.* New York: Robert M. McBride & Company, 1923. Internet Archive, 2019. https://archive.org/details/fairytalesfromor00mart/page/n7/mode/2up.

The Disowned Princess
Martens, Frederick H. Edited by Dr. R. Wilhelm. *The Chinese Fairy Book.* New York: Frederick A Stokes Company, 1921. Internet Archive, 2007. https://archive.org/details/chinesefairybook00wilhrich/page/n7/mode/2up.

The Fisherman and His Wife
Grimm, Jacob and Wilhelm. Translated and edited by Margaret Hunt. *Grimm's Household Tales.* London: George Bell and Sons, 1884. Internet Archive, 2009. https://archive.org/details/grimmshouseholdt01grim/page/n3/mode/2up.

The Fisherman and the Draug
Lie, Jonas. Translated by R. Nisbet Bain. *Weird Tales from Northern Seas.* London: Kegan Paul, Trench, Trubner & Co. Ltd., 1893. Internet Archive, 2008. https://archive.org/details/weirdtalesfromn00liegoog.

Kae's Theft of the Whale

Grey, Sir George. *Polynesian Mythology and Ancient Traditional History of the New Zealand Race, as Furnished by Their Priests and Chiefs*. London: John Murray, 1855. Internet Archive, 2017. https://archive.org/details/in.ernet.dli.2015.219427/page/n3/mode/2up.

Kahalaopuna, Princess of Manoa

Thrum, Thos. G. *Hawaiian Folk Tales: A Collection of Native Legends*. Chicago: A. C. McClurg & Co., 1907. Internet Archive, 2008. https://archive.org/details/hawaiianfolktale00thru/page/n14/mode/2up.

The Mermaid's Vengeance

Hunt, Robert. *Popular Romances of the West of England, or the Drolls, Traditions, and Superstitions of Old Cornwall*. London: Chatto & Windus, 1908. Internet Archive, 2007. https://archive.org/details/popularromanceso00huntuoft/page/n5/mode/2up.

The Merman

Arnason, Jón. *Icelandic Legends*. Translated by George E. J. Powell and Eiríkur Magnússon. London: Richard Bentley 1864. Internet Archive, 2009. https://archive.org/details/icelandiclegend02powegoog.

The Old Man Who Became a Fish

Bang, Im, Yi Ryuk, and Anon. Translated by James S. Gale. *Korean Folk Tales*. London and New York: J. M. Dent & Sons and E. P. Dutton & Co., 1913. Internet Archive, 2007. https://archive.org/details/koreanfolktalesi00impaiala/page/n6/mode/2up.

Origin of the Narwhal

Boas, Franz. "The Central Eskimo." Washington: *Bureau of Ethnology Sixth Annual Report*, pl. II, Smithsonian Institution, 1888. Project Gutenberg, 2013. http://www.gutenberg.org/files/42084/42084-h/42084-h.htm#tales_narwhal.

The Story of Urashima Taro, the Fisher Lad

Ozaki, Yei Theodora. *Japanese Fairy Tales*. New York: Grosset & Dunlap, 1908. Internet Archive, 2007. https://archive.org/details/japanesefairytal00ozak.

The Three Copecks

Ralston, W. R. S. *Russian Fairy Tales: A Choice Collection of Muscovite Folk-Lore.* New York: Pollard & Moss, 1887. Internet Archive, 2012. https://archive.org/details/russianfairytale00rals/page/n4/mode/2up.

Thunder and Anansi

Barker, W. H. and Cecilia Sinclair. *West African Folk-Tales.* London: George G. Harrap & Company, 1917. Internet Archive, 2008. https://archive.org/details/westafricanfolkt00barkrich/page/n8/mode/2up.

Tom Moore and the Seal Woman

Curtin, Jeremiah. *Tales of the Fairies and of the Ghost World.* Boston: Little, Brown & Company 1895. Internet Archive, 2009. https://archive.org/details/talesfairiesand00curtgoog/page/n9.